OLD FRIENDS AND NEW, ANOTHER MURDER

A Sheridan Hendley Mystery

CHRISTA NARDI

Cover Design by Brenda Walter

Other Books with Sheridan Hendley

The Cold Creek Series by Christa Nardi:
Murder at Cold Creek College (Cold Creek #1)
Murder in the Arboretum (Cold Creek #2)
Murder at the Grill (Cold Creek #3)
Murder in the Theater (Cold Creek #4)
Murder and a Wedding (Cold Creek #5

Sheridan Hendley Mysteries by Christa Nardi:
A New Place, Another Murder (A Sheridan Hendley Mystery #1)
Dogs and More Dogs, Another Murder (A Sheridan Hendley Mystery #2)
Old Friends and New, Another Murder (A Sheridan Hendley Mystery #3)
Holly and Mistletoe, Another Murder (A Sheridan Hendley Mystery #4) – Coming in 2020

CHAPTER 1

Charlie and Bella's barking and pawing woke me up. Even a little disgruntled, I couldn't help but smile at the antics of my older Sheltie and the young lab mix. The smell of coffee helped, too.

A glance at the clock and I groaned. I had overslept. Again. With the weekend over, work beckoned, at least three days a week at my continuing temporary job at Millicent College. That and the joys of getting one teenager up and ready for high school.

Grumbling to myself, I checked Maddie's room on my way to the kitchen. She didn't answer the knock on her door, so I opened it and shooed the dogs inside. She screeched and I chuckled. Definitely not a morning person. Her typical teen concern for her appearance slowed her down even more whenever she had to leave the house.

"Come on, Maddie. You need to get a move on."

In the kitchen, Brett was absorbed in something on his tablet. Although we were no longer newlyweds, nothing was better than waking up to this man, with his hazel eyes, dark curly hair, contagious smile, and dimples. A six-foot teddy bear unless on the job as a State Police detective or in protective mode.

He quickly shifted the screen on the tablet and smiled.

"Work already? Anything interesting?"

"Not really."

Maddie stumbled into the kitchen. At fifteen, she was a feminine version of her father, with long, dark hair and hazel eyes. With her last growth spurt, she was almost as tall as me. To her dismay, that made her taller than most of the boys in her grade, including her close friend, Alex.

"Maddie, stand up straight. You look great. Got all your homework?" Brett handed her a glass of orange juice as he spoke and kissed her forehead.

"Thanks." A quick glance at her watch and she emptied the glass. "Gotta run." She grabbed her coat and raced out the door, her backpack slung over her shoulder.

Brett shook his head and smiled. "She's grown up so fast."

"For sure, and that learner's permit is burning a hole in her wallet. In no time, she'll be driving."

His jaw dropped and his eyes widened. "I'm not ready for that. Or boys who drive."

The ring tone of his phone interrupted his train of thought. Work. I bustled around the kitchen and made myself a bagel. I waved one at him and he shook his head as he stashed his phone and grabbed his tablet.

"Fabry. We need to go to North Shore. Something's come up and we need to check it out." He leaned over, kissed me, and stole a bite of my bagel. "Later."

I nodded. Detective James Fabry was his partner when something bigger than the ordinary assignments locally came up. That "something" often translated to a dead body or major drug bust or similar. Assigned to Division III in Appomattox, Brett and Fabry often caught the situations outside of the immediate area. Like Brett, Fabry had been with the State Police for many years, though he was the older and more cynical of the two.

Brett and I met when he was assigned to the murder of one of my colleagues in Cold Creek. I smiled as I recalled my time in Cold Creek, meeting Brett, and our friends. Cold Creek wasn't that far away from Clover Hill where we lived now.

Charlie's nose nudged me out of my dreams. Brett had already fed both dogs and I let them out. The temperature had dropped, not unexpected for a fall day. A quick glance at the thermometer of our weather station assured me it was chilly, but not yet cold. I poured myself another cup of coffee, settled the dogs in, and, as usual, was the last to leave the house.

Like Maddie, with everything I needed was in my backpack. A quick stop at the Starbucks drive through and I was on my way. The ride through the hills from Clover Hill to the college was beautiful, the leaves on the trees beginning to turn. In the winter, the drive got a little tricky with possible black ice, especially on the two bridges. For now, I enjoyed the kaleidoscope of color and sunlight.

Millicent College was a small liberal arts college like Cold Creek College. Originally, a women's college that changed in the 70s though no one at the college seemed to remember that earlier time. Least not that I had met. This was my second year as a Visiting Assistant Professor and it suited me.

Unlike my position at Cold Creek College, my only responsibility was to teach assigned classes and attend a meeting or two. Like semi-retirement, though I still had a few years before I reached fifty. This schedule fit my new life style, leaving me with plenty of time for Brett and Maddie, as well as to volunteer at the local dog rescue, Clover Hill Pets & Paws.

I arrived early for a change, walking in with Dr. Addison, the Psychology Department Head. About my age, he had reddish blonde hair and a moustache, set off with blue eyes. His wool trench coat in deference to the weather reminded me of old westerns and made me smile.

"Good morning, Dr. Hendley. You seem in a good mood this brisk morning."

"I am. How are you this morning?"

"Good. Busy. Meetings and paperwork. Semester seems to be going well. Enrollment is up and the trustees are happy." He hesitated and added, "Hopefully, the faculty and staff are as well."

I smiled as we reached the hall where his suite of offices was located. He nodded and disappeared, and I ducked into the large lounge area and refilled my coffee from the Keurig machine. Coffee in hand, I stopped at my office to drop things off and then was in teaching mode.

I nodded and smiled at colleagues and students as I made my way back to my friend, Keurig, after class. As usual, the lounge was bustling with activity and noise, students, staff, and faculty alike. It was lunch time and the fast food venues had long lines. I got in line and watched the big screen as I waited.

A running announcement on the bottom of the screen indicated "Breaking News: State Police make a concerning discovery in North Shore, VA." That was it. No details. And then the announcements shifted to report sports scores.

Frustrated, I checked my phone but there were no messages from Brett. No doubt he and Fabry were preoccupied with whatever had been discovered. My curiosity was killing me.

CHAPTER 2

The first message from Brett was not unexpected. He was still in North Shore and we should eat without him. I stopped at Seafood Grill and Deli and picked up a wide assortment of salads and sides. Maddie's favorite and easy enough for Brett to snack on when he got home. Fabry, too, if he came by.

I no sooner got home and let the dogs out, and Maddie walked in, phone in hand.

"What?" "Really?" "I haven't heard." As she disconnected, she looked at me. "Alex beat me home. He said it's on the news. A murder in North Shore. Dad's there, isn't he?"

My jaw dropped and I turned on the television to catch the news, choosing KCCX, the Cold Creek station, over our local one. "That's where he and Fabry were going this morning. He texted he'd be late, but not why."

We ate our dinner and waited for more information. It was minimal and to the point. A man was murdered in North Shore and they'd share information as it became available.

"We know what your dad's been up to all day. How was your day?"

"Good, though I have a lot of homework and choir practice two days this week." She shook her head. "There's other stuff I want to do, but no time. I thought about track and Coach Kamin spoke to me about it, but there's no way."

"Decision time. You have to plan out your week and figure out what you can fit in and then prioritize. I'm not an athlete, but I'd think track would mean practices every day and some meets would be away. That means missing some days of school. Sport is a big commitment."

"I think I nixed that one when she mentioned something about the team running first thing in the morning – like before school." Her open mouth and raised eyebrows communicated just how unbelievable she found that concept. I burst out laughing.

"Maybe you should stick to choir, then. A couple extra after school or evening rehearsals isn't quite so painful. And you like singing and performing, right?"

"Oh, yeah. We're already planning for the winter concert. Mr. Contralto wants us to come up with an eclectic something or other. What does that mean?"

"Usually it means a combination of different approaches or perspectives. Perhaps in this case, something classical, something popular, something jazzy, something rap… or some pieces that are wintry and some that are more holiday centered?"

She nodded and smiled, her eyes twinkling. "That would be better than the same old, same old. Shake things up a bit."

She finished eating, helped clean up our plates, and disappeared into her room. I smiled, knowing full well her efforts would be split between homework and Alex and her friend, Nedra. Maddie was a great student and motivated to do well in school. We were lucky.

The phone ringing interrupted my reflections on Maddie as a teen.

"Hi, Kim. How are you?"

Kim Pennzel was my close friend from Cold Creek. We'd worked together for almost six years and stayed in touch when I'd married Brett and moved to Clover Hill. Although a few years younger than me, we shared backgrounds – both psychologists, both divorced. Kim always had a lot more energy than me and sometimes acted on impulse. We talked a lot and often she and Marty would come to Clover Hill or we would go there.

As usual, she was excited. I shrugged as she began to babble.

"Is Brett involved in the murder? I can't believe another murder. You know, he's welcome to stay with us if he needs to be here overnight. Has he told you anything yet?"

I'd managed to get involved in a few mysteries along the way, and she was my sidekick of sorts. I chuckled. "Brett and Fabry are in North Shore. All he's told me is that he'd be late. Thanks for the offer to put him up. I'll pass it along. What do you know?"

North Shore is a small town like Cold Creek and only about thirty minutes away from the college. When I lived in Cold Creek, it was sometimes a nice change to go to dinner up there or to Alta Vista, another small town the same distance away.

"Marty and I were going to go to dinner at the new brewpub up there – Leavitt's, but when I mentioned it to Chief Hirsch, he said the road was closed. Actually, he suggested we go to Alta Vista instead. The news didn't say much else, but that one section of the road from Cold Creek to North Shore is closed. The newscaster showed a map of how to get to the center of town going around the main highway. That looked crazy. How long can they keep virtually the only direct road from Cold Creek to North Shore closed? Max is beside himself."

Max Bentley was another colleague from Cold Creek, mostly annoying, with big ambitions. A bit like the stereotypic professor, he had black hair, that was perpetually messy, papers always in disarray, and stormed around like he was in charge, yet confused at the same time. More recently, he'd applied to be department head. Kim had shared he was resentful he didn't get the position and was giving the new person a lot of grief.

"At least he can't blame this one on me."

Kim laughed. "No, but that didn't stop the hysteria. He recently moved out of Cold Creek and closer to North Shore. He was ranting and raving with his wife on the phone about security and bad neighbors or something. I think he's regretting his move. Buying the new house? His way of saving face. The pictures are beautiful. Come to think of it, if the road's closed, I'm not sure he can get home."

"And wait until he finds out Brett is there."

We both laughed. Max was intimidated by Brett early on, and though he came to terms with him, they were never going to be best friends. Kim and I chatted for a little longer and she caught me up on the Cold Creek gossip in no time.

"Kim, Brett just pulled in and it looks like James is with him. I'll talk to you later."

I pulled out more plates, serving utensils, and the food as the men walked in. Brett smiled and nodded as I popped a pod into the Keurig machine.

Brett pointed down the hall and as Fabry disappeared, he pulled me to him and gave me a kiss. "Nasty situation. Maddie?"

"Homework in her room."

He nodded and headed in that direction. James joined me in the kitchen and I handed him a cup of coffee. "Help yourself."

He nodded. "Long day and short on food."

He attacked the food like he hadn't eaten in days. I was glad I'd picked up extra of everything. Just in case, I fixed a hearty plate for Brett. He joined us, Charlie and Bella following, and he let the dogs out before he sat down.

"How was your day? Anything exciting at Millicent?"

"Not really. The leaves are turning though and the drive through the hills was awesome. They haven't peaked yet though, so I'll get to enjoy the drive for another week or so."

He nodded. "That sounds about right. I bet they're changing in Sleepy Hollow as well. We may have to go running there next weekend and take it all in. If not there, then somewhere."

Fabry cleared his throat. "That assumes we have this wrapped up by then. I'm not so sure."

CHAPTER 3

My curiosity had been piqued all day, not that I planned on getting involved. I had enough to do here in Clover Hill. "Who was murdered? What happened?"

The two men exchanged glances and James shrugged. Brett nodded.

"A call came in from someone who explained they'd been camping up there, near the lake, and on their hike found a man, dead. The caller was told to stay there and wait for the first responder out of North Shore on the closest stretch of road. You remember Tally? He took over after the drug busts there. He responded, but there was no one on the road. A flare had been lit at one spot and that was where he stopped and called for help."

"And that would be us and our friend, Jeff - Chief Hirsch - from Cold Creek, and Matt Sutherland, local police from Alta Vista. Only it's fall and everything is lush, and yes, changing colors. No obvious, well-used path near the flare."

"A prank?"

Brett shrugged. "When someone reports a body in the woods, we search for any signs. And that's what we did most of the day. Thankfully, it wasn't hot and the trees provided a lot of shade."

"Also meant we had to use flashlights and step carefully."

"But you obviously found the body. It's been on the news."

"We spread out on either side of the flare and tried to find some indication of how the flare got there. Whoever called it in – and they're still trying to track that – apparently drove to where they thought would be the place on the road? Or intentionally made it difficult. We called in the K-9 unit after thrashing in the woods for a while."

"Two dogs and their partners came and Tally suggested we should try from a known campsite, even though it wasn't in line with the flare, while they worked from the flare. Long story short – we met about halfway between the flare and the campground. There was definitely evidence of more than one camper, and some indications they'd been hunting, out of season of course."

"Probably why they left before you got there. Wanting to alert someone of their find, but not wanting to get arrested?"

"Good point, Sher. That's one possibility. When we saw shell-casings at the campsite, we wondered if they'd killed the man by accident."

Fabry added his thoughts. "Only the man had been dead for a while. The coroner will figure out the time element. From the campsite and garbage, the campers had only been there two nights at most. A weekend camping and hunting weekend. Maybe they shot him Saturday and didn't find him until today. Or someone else shot him before that and they stumbled on him today."

"Has he been identified? Reported missing?"

Brett smiled and lifted his hand to me to tell me to stop. "He wasn't there camping nor was he in a business suit. Nice pants, polo shirt. Casual. His wallet was thrown from his body – one of the dogs found it first. Tally was going to pay a visit to the address on his driver's license. We waited for the rest of the crew coming in to take care of evidence and transport the body."

"Was he dumped there?"

"Not clear yet. He was a few feet from the path, his foot the only thing visible from the path, if you were looking at it. The ground cover showed some trampling there. Possibly from whoever found him, possibly from being dragged to that spot, or both. I checked the pants legs and not a lot of dirt I could see. Tests will tell us more, but I think he was killed there, either that or carried to the spot where the trail and woods meet. And that would be a long carry or drag with no indication anything had been dragged."

Fabry nodded as he finished speaking and reached for more food. Brett nodded as well and finished off the coleslaw.

"I'm guessing you two didn't get lunch, huh?" We all laughed. "Anything else going on?"

"We can only speculate on the murder until we get more information. It may not even require our presence and then we can definitely go hiking and see the foliage this weekend."

Other than when called in for assistance, the State Police tended to let local law enforcement handle their own cases. State Police involvement long term usually was limited to activities that could cross county or state lines, no local crime.

"Well, Kim called and given how close she and Marty are, she said if you need a place to crash, to let her know."

They nodded. "Be sure to thank her for the offer, but I'm hoping we are done after tomorrow. Local problem."

"She also mentioned Max was hysterical. To make up for not getting the department head job, he moved toward North Shore."

Brett turned to Fabry. "He's another reason I really hope this is a local problem. Don't get me wrong, Max has shown he has good points. On the other hand, his arrogance and flamboyant personality get on my nerves. I'll never understand how his wife, Stella, puts up with his antics." He shook his head.

"Sounds like a real character. I almost hope I get to meet him."

Fabry stood as he spoke. Brett laughed. "I'll pick you up at 7 o'clock. Good night, Sheridan, and thanks for the food."

After Fabry left, Brett helped me clean up and Maddie came out of her room for a snack.

"A murder, Dad?"

He nodded. "I'm hoping it is all resolved tomorrow, definitely by the end of the week. How about a weekend in Sleepy Hollow or some place to go hiking and enjoy the fall weather and colors?"

Multiple expressions crossed Maddie's face in rapid succession. Brett looked from me to her as if he was afraid she was ill.

"What's the problem, Maddie?"

"It sounds great, but… the whole weekend? Don't we need to help out at Pets & Paws? I'm sure I'll have lots of homework. And Alex… Nedra may need my help."

Brett's mouth dropped and his eyebrows arched. I tried not to laugh.

"What's so funny?"

"I think your daughter is trying to – as diplomatically as she can – let us know that plans for the 'whole weekend' could interfere with her social life."

His shoulders slumped. "That right, Maddie?"

She nodded and shuffled her feet. "I love you, Dad. You too, Sher. But my friends, you know…"

With that she walked back to her room, shaking her head, snack forgotten. I pulled Brett toward me. He looked so forlorn.

"I'm so not ready for this, Sher. She's grown up too fast this past year."

I nodded and managed to distract him, at least for a while.

CHAPTER 4

As I drove out to the local shelter, Pets & Paws, something my mother used to say popped into my head. "If it's Tuesday, we must be in Belgium." She said it had something to do with month long tours through Europe when she was younger. We'd talked on Sunday and she was excited about taking a cruise sponsored by the housing association. She and my dad were looking forward to it. And that made me feel good.

I was still smiling as I walked into Pets & Paws and Susie waved.

"Hey, Sheridan. Glad to see you. Mrs. Chantilly had some appointments this morning and I'm the only one here until Luke gets out of school."

Susie was also a volunteer, though it was somehow connected with her studies to become a veterinary technician. Today, she had a blue streak in her blonde hair, blue scrubs, and tennis shoes. Luke was now officially a volunteer, however, he'd started at Pets & Paws as part of his probation and the community service requirement.

"What can I do to help?"

"Can you work the back area with the bigger dogs while I do the others? Just holler if you need any help. There's a new one – dumped and brought in yesterday. She just hovers in the corner. Sad."

Shaking my head, I pursed my lips. "I'll see what I can do. Coffee made?"

Susie laughed. "You bet. We planned on you coming in."

Mrs. Chantilly owned Pets & Paws and lived upstairs. A unique individual, she didn't quite conform to social norms. The shelter part of the house was the downstairs of the older home. I stashed my stuff in the kitchen, grabbed a cup of coffee, and headed to the back area of the house. Probably the area that would have been called the "great room" or "living room" depending on who was describing it.

The larger dogs in larger crates all greeted me. Well, all but one. She looked to be part lab, with a mostly chocolate coat. The white swirls amidst the chocolate reminded me of hot chocolate. Obviously someone agreed and she was named "Cocoa" on the clipboard.

I kneeled down and talked to her quietly and let her smell my hand. She was skinny and likely malnourished, but not obviously injured. After a few minutes, I moved on and started the routine with her neighbor, Golden. She was a mixed breed, part retriever, and her name reflected the prominent color of her coat. I leashed her and took her out the back door into the dog run.

While she enjoyed a much larger area to run around in, I cleaned out her crate, replaced her blanket, and refilled her water and food dishes. That done, I played a quick game of catch, toweled her off with a damp towel, and it was back in the crate for her. She knew the routine as well as I did. There were only eight big ones, so I could take my time with them. As I finished with each one, I stopped by Cocoa's crate and talked to her some more.

Mid-morning and half way done, I took a break. I found Susie in her favorite place – the mama and puppies area. This was also Maddie's favorite. There was one mama and pups today. Then I noticed something.

"Susie, I don't remember the cream-colored pups and there seem to be more instead of less?"

"The pups were rescued. The mama didn't make it. Lolita here is helping out as best she can and I'm bottle feeding them. Not sure what breed or breeds, but they are cute. We could sure use Maddie's help."

She smiled and handed me one of the cream bundles. He was barely bigger than my hand and very squirmy. I laughed as it took me two hands to hold on to him. We chatted for a while, and then I got back to work.

I saved Cocoa for last. After my break, she seemed to be watching me as I worked the room. I kept up the routine of stopping to talk to her as I finished with one dog and before the next one. A little concerned she might not come out of the crate or that she'd bolt, I positioned myself on the floor in front of the gate as I opened it. I cleaned the floor of the crate near the door and pulled out the food and water bowls.

As I talked to her in what I hoped was a soothing tone, I gently and slowly pulled the blanket with her on it toward me. She lifted her head and her tail thumped once. Taking that as a good sign, I continued to work her out of the crate and onto the floor. Poor girl needed a bath. Once she was standing and leashed, we went out the back door.

She spotted the dog run and backed off. I soothed her. I could only imagine that she had been left in something like that too often. Hooking her leash to a longer plastic chain, I popped back inside to get some shampoo. She sat at the door and waited.

I turned on the water and let it run. That didn't seem to scare her and I was able to get her bathed and toweled off. Inside, I attached her leash to a clip on the wall and she sat there while I cleaned her crate, gave her a new blanket, and fresh food and water. She nudged me and put her head on my lap.

"You seem to have made friends with Miss Cocoa there. A sorry state if ever. How are you, Sheridan? You and your handsome man involved in that murder?"

I smiled at Mrs. Chantilly, not quite sure what "look" she was trying for today. She sported a wide-brimmed black hat, a black shift and white vest. A pilgrim came to mind, though Thanksgiving was still six weeks away.

"I'm good. FYI, Cocoa here is leery of the run. But yes, I think we're now friends." I scooted her toward the crate and removed the leash.

"No worries, Cocoa. Luke or somebody will get you out again later and I'll be back."

"What about the murder? It's all Blake could talk about. None of the Buchanans are involved are they?"

The Buchanan family, and especially Blake, had a lot of clout in Clover Hill and the surrounding area. And they'd been involved in one murder right after Brett and I got married, as well as drugs. That had been the reason Luke was assigned community service.

"Brett hasn't said much about it. But it happened in North Shore. Any of the Buchanans live out that way?"

The Buchanans had a long history in Clover Hill with eight brothers as founding fathers. Most of them had left the area, but with each generation the family ties covered more and more of the state. Many of the region's political leaders were members of the Buchanan clan.

"You know, we might need to redo the floors and paint in here if we ever have enough room to move these dogs to the front of the house."

Anyone else switching topics, I'd be suspicious. With Mrs. Chantilly, it wasn't unusual though. It happened all the time. The floors were concrete and had been sealed and stained. With metal crates and dog nails, there was some wear evident. I nodded.

"Could definitely do with a complete washing again if nothing else. Maybe you could identify a Saturday when all of us volunteers could come in and get as many dogs outside at once."

"You are always full of good ideas. Rehomed so many dogs. Yes, we need to do that. I'll put Luke in charge. He's grown up so much don't you think?"

I smiled and nodded. Before she started reminiscing, I made a hasty exit. "Let me know when. In the meantime, I have shopping to do."

She didn't respond and was telling Cocoa about Luke when I left.

CHAPTER 5

The house was quiet when I finally made it home to let Charlie and Bella out. I unloaded the car and fixed dinner. Given Fabry's appetite the night before, I'd decided on a pot roast and got it in the oven. It seemed eerily quiet and I turned on Pandora for some music as I prepped for my classes later in the week. Alerts beeped on my smart watch just as it rang.

"Hi, Kim. What's up?"

"You won't believe it, Sheridan. Max has gone off the deep end. They identified the man who was killed. His name was Connor Landry. Apparently, he lived in the same subdivision as Max."

"Did Max know him? Is that why he's upset?" With Max, it could be anything or nothing that got him upset. I was hoping for a more logical explanation.

"Yes, he knew him. Ali told me – Hirsch told her – Max had a screaming argument with the man a few weeks ago. Accused the man of flirting with Stella and walking his dog to their house on purpose to see her. And not even cleaning up after his dog."

"Wait. This Connor person was Max's neighbor? And Max got mad because he thought the man was after his wife?"

"Yup. And he knows Brett is up there and he's ranting about how Brett's wanted to pin a murder on him since Adam."

Brett and I met when my colleague, Adam Millberg, was murdered in the sports center on campus. Max was condescending and tried to dismiss Brett. It hadn't gone well. They had words and neither ever forgot. Max was a hot head and control freak. He also had a heart of gold, but that isn't usually what people saw.

"Brett is not after him. He never was. Max acts guilty with his attitude and refuses to talk to them or loses his temper… This could be bad. Has Brett or Fabry shown up on campus? Even tried to talk to him?"

"Not yet. Terra's husband, Joe has been around asking questions. Somehow he got wind of it. And, …" She chuckled. "Sher, your name has come up a few times."

Terra was the mainstay in the department though as staff her efforts and those of the other staff member were often overlooked or taken for granted.

Joe, her husband, worked for the local paper, such that it was.

"In a good way, I hope."

"In a 'we have another mystery – where's Sheridan' way. So when are you coming to town? Everyone is asking. We all know you won't be able to stay away if Max is a suspect."

I laughed. My curiosity about murders had gotten me into some tight spots in Cold Creek and since. "Hold on. This could all be resolved quickly and have nothing to do with Max. Max isn't violent – he just doesn't have a lot of self-control."

I hesitated as I repeated what I said. He was short on impulse control and lost his temper easily.

"Sheridan, you slowed down as you talked and now you're not talking at all."

"Just thinking. No, Max is not the type to plan a murder. And I can't imagine him in the woods. His pants would get dirty and he might get bit by a bug. Sure, he has a short temper and rants and waves his arms, but actually kill somebody? I don't think so. Not unless he's gotten worse."

It was Kim's turn to laugh. "Well?"

"I'll see what's happening. I don't teach on Thursday, so that's a possibility. Whole thing may blow over by then."

My phone signaled another call, also from Cold Creek. "I have another call. I'll talk to you later."

I disconnected and connected.

"Hello?"

"Oh my gosh, Sheridan. You won't believe what happened. I don't believe it. And your husband. He's here and he's going to arrest me. After all I did for you in the past. You can't possibly believe I'd kill someone. I couldn't even kill the mice in my lab when my studies ended. I had to get the students to take care of them. You have to convince your husband, okay?"

He paused long enough to catch a breath. If his speech rate was any indication, his blood pressure had to be sky high.

"Hi, Max. Take a deep breath or two. Calm down. Why would anyone think you killed someone?"

"My neighbor was killed. I'm sure you heard it on the news. Are you trying to trick me? I know that's what police do all the time. Ask you a question they already know the answer to. I watch *Law and Order* you know."

"Good show. And I do know someone was murdered in North Shore. It's been on the news. But how would I know he was your neighbor. Even the new notification I got a few minutes ago with the victim's name didn't tell me who his neighbors were."

"Okay, so maybe you didn't know. But your husband's always been out to get me and now he's going to arrest me. I think he's jealous of me, I really do."

I rolled my eyes and was thankful he couldn't see my expression.

"Max, are you guilty?"

"What? How could you even ask that question after knowing me for so long? What did I ever do to you?"

"Max, if you're not guilty and you just answer whatever questions Chief Hirsch or anyone else – including Brett – asks, it will work out. If you're worried, find yourself an attorney to advise you."

"I'll ask that attorney who worked for the hostess at the Grill. Do you know his name? And Joe? He's asking lots of questions, too, and isn't that a violation of my rights somehow? I'm sure it is."

I shook my head even though he couldn't see it. At least he saved me from having to answer his question and giving him Marty's number.

"You don't have to answer Joe's questions. He can ask them and you choose to answer or not. He's a reporter, not a policeman."

"Okay. Okay."

"Max, I need to get off the phone and check on dinner. It was good talking with you."

He disconnected without another word and I stared at my phone. No doubt about it, Max was a being unto himself.

My phone rang again. Brett.

"Hi, Sher. We're going to stay the night here. There are a few complications and we plan to start ironing out the wrinkles first thing in the morning."

"Are you going to stay in North Shore or take Kim up on the offer in Cold Creek?"

"Here. We have a lot of reports and information to process. We'll stay at the only hotel here. It's not quite as quaint as the one in Alta Vista though. We'll hash out what we have and what information we need while we eat dinner. I'll give you a call later. Okay?"

"Not a problem. Pot roast was on the menu and I'm sure there will be leftovers."

"Tempting me with one of my favorite meals. Not fair. Later. Love you."

CHAPTER 6

The shower felt good, Maddie was asleep, and Charlie and I were in bed reading a mystery novel. Without Brett, the bed seemed much bigger. I laughed as my phone chimed at the same time I thought of him.

"How's it going? Did you figure it all out?"

"No such luck. The time of death? Best guess is sometime between Thursday and Saturday. No one is quite sure why there wasn't more, uh, damage to the body from animals. James and I? We think because he wasn't moved there until Saturday and the camper-hunter folks made enough noise, the animals stayed away."

"That would make sense. You said it didn't look like he'd been dragged. Carried would make more sense then. Or killed there. Was he shot?"

"Yes. Three times. Small caliber gun. They did retrieve two bullets. No quick match in the system. A full search to see if that gun has been tested before will take a long time."

"I guess I'm relieved he was shot. Max called me, all upset."

"I imagine he is. He started ranting as soon as he spotted me. I tried to blame it on James, but that didn't fly. I plan to keep my distance though I think he spotted me today."

"Max thinks you want to arrest him for this man's murder?"

"All I can say is that Max Bentley is among the persons of interest in the case. We are working our way down the list. I know you work tomorrow at Millicent. Any chance you could come to Cold Creek on Thursday? He might be more amenable to talking if you're here. Or maybe you can at least keep him calm."

"Kim suggested the same thing. I can drive down in the morning, but have to be back at Millicent on Friday. I'll check with Melina and see if Maddie can stay there in case it's late on Thursday when I – or we – get home. I don't really think my being there will help, though."

"Probably not, but you also might pick up on something we miss. And I don't mean just from him."

"What else?" I sat up, jostling Charlie as I did.

"Do you remember Jared Skinner? Sebastian Cabot? Names ring a bell?"

"Vaguely. Drugs is the only connection I remember and somehow connected to Justin Blake's murder. Skinner any way. Not sure I remember Cabot."

"Right. Connor Landry's family is very close with the Cabots. In our conversation with Landry's widow, she mentioned her husband met with Sebastian Cabot and a Chase Jarvit for dinner on Thursday evening and again for breakfast on Friday morning. From what she said, the three families – Landry, Cabot, and Jarvit – often socialized. The men were close and went back some time."

"Did he make those meetings? Wouldn't that narrow the time of death?"

"Yes to dinner. And he did go home Thursday night. Mrs. Landry said he was gone when she got up around 9 o'clock, her assumption being he went to meet the other two for breakfast."

"And?"

He chuckled. "He never showed for breakfast. Cabot and Jarvit waited for him, ate breakfast, and left. We confirmed that."

"Ahh, so he was alive until he left the house Friday morning. At least that narrows the time frame for you and the suspects. Where did they go for dinner and breakfast? The local options aren't that great."

"North Shore has added a few food options. There's even a new brewpub type place. Brew their own beer. James and I ate there tonight and confirmed that the three men ate there on Thursday. As far as the help was concerned, the three men had a pleasant meal, nothing out of the ordinary."

"Kim mentioned something about that place. She and Marty were going there last night, only the road was closed."

"Open now. Breakfast was at a small organic diner. The Eggspot."

"Organic? Okay. Did you breakfast there?"

He laughed. "Heck, no. Place was jammed and only open from 5 a.m. to 2 p.m. We did chat with the owner and wait staff and perused the menu."

"And?"

"You wouldn't like the food. Not just because it's organic, but it's also over the top with tofu and soy and sauces; there's not much plain on the menu. And you can only deconstruct a menu item so much to get it plain. Besides, they don't serve coffee or expresso. Only herbal teas."

I groaned. Definitely not my type of place.

"What about the breakfast meeting?"

"Cabot, Jarvit, and Landry ate there frequently. The waiter was surprised Landry didn't show up. Described Landry as the most down to earth of the three. And the best tipper."

"Cabot or Jarvit have a motive?"

"We're, uh, looking into both of them. A 'red flag' popped up when I visited Jarvit's office and ran into Jared Skinner leaving. Only Jarvit wasn't there so I couldn't ask him about it. With Skinner around, I have to think drugs again."

Only a few years ago, there'd been a big drug bust in North Shore and a related murder in Cold Creek.

Jared Skinner had been involved, was arrested, and went to jail.

"You'll keep chasing the information up in North Shore tomorrow and then branch out, like to Max, on Thursday?"

"That's the plan. Any new information could change that. Despite Max's tirade when Tally, the police officer from North Shore, questioned him, I am not out to hang a murder on him. But even Max admits having a very loud disagreement with Landry over dog poop."

I snorted. "That is too funny."

"What are your plans for tomorrow?"

"Teaching in the morning. I'll get in touch with Melina about Thursday and over the weekend for Maddie, if we can get away. You know, friendships are very fragile with teen girls. I sure hope Maddie and Nedra stay friends for a long time. And Maddie should have Nedra over sometimes, so it's not always Melina and Vincent with the extra person."

"Good points. Fabry is giving me signals to shut up already. He needs his beauty sleep."

"Okay, g'nite. Hope you can get home tomorrow night, with this case closed."

We disconnected and I hoped Landry's death wasn't just a local problem. I didn't know Tally, and I liked Hirsch, but my experiences in Cold Creek with Chief Pfeiffe didn't give me a lot of confidence when it came to local police officials in small towns.

CHAPTER 7

Teaching was the last thing on my mind as I made my way to Millicent College. My head was buzzing with what little information I had on the murder and the possible drug angle. It didn't help that a news brief mentioned both a faculty member at Cold Creek College and drugs in the same sentence. For all that makes Max who he is, drugs? Nope.

I almost frowned when I spotted Dr. Addison, however I quickly replaced it with a smile.

"Good Morning, Dr. Addison. How are you?"

"I'm fine, Sheridan. I heard on the news about the problems down in Cold Creek and North Shore. You don't have anything to do with that, do you? Did you know the faculty member they think is responsible?"

"I know as much as you do. There have been a few new faculty and others left. It's possible I know their 'person of interest,' of course." I smiled my most innocent smile as I skirted the truth.

He nodded his head. "We don't want any of that stuff filtering up here. We dealt with the drug issue back when you identified the dealers. Millicent College doesn't need any more untoward publicity. It upsets the Trustees."

"I understand. I will not do anything to reflect badly on Millicent."

And I could say that honestly, though I suspected that eliminating Luke and Caleb as dealers and pushers, and putting Shane Buchanan in jail, didn't mean someone else hadn't shown up to fill their positions. Where there were consumers, there would be new suppliers to provide the goods.

He smiled and nodded as he walked away. My suspicious mind wondered if he planned to meet me in the parking lot each day or if it was a coincidence this week. I shook my head at the ridiculousness of the thought. After all, no one knew anything on Monday morning.

Backpack in hand, my next stop was the Keurig machine. One of the other faculty, Leah Buxbaum, tapped my arm as she passed me.

"Coffeecake and muffins in the lounge – homemade. You don't want to miss it." She smiled and headed in that direction. Leah's office was next to mine, though somewhat bigger, and she shared my love of coffee. She taught sociology and criminology, not all that removed from psychology.

The faculty lounge or break room was not a place I frequented, except when the Keurig lines were too long in the larger lounge. The Mr. Coffee machine was a last, desperate choice for me. Coffeecake sounded good though. I hoped it was cinnamon or cream cheese, my two favorites, and I was not disappointed. Someone had made a cream cheese filled coffeecake with cinnamon and pecans. It looked and smelled delish.

Grabbing a piece, I realized the topic of conversation was the murder and decided to sit down. I only knew a few of the faculty as a part-time adjunct, but smiled at the few I recognized. And tried not to stare at the man who seemed to be holding court. Him, I didn't know.

Dr. Austin Antos, as I learned later, recently joined the faculty, replacing a faculty member who died suddenly. That faculty member had taught economics and finance. My best guess put him in his thirties. Jet black hair, in curls to his shoulder, light brown skin, and eyes so blue he had to be wearing colored contact lenses. He smiled and his whole face lit up. And it was a very handsome face setting off an athletic build emphasized by his snug polo shirt.

"Austin, of course it's just terrible. Forget all the psychology mumbo jumbo. What do you think, you know, from an economics perspective?" The cute blonde leaned toward him as she spoke, as did several of the others. I glanced around the room and Leah rolled her eyes. It was hard not to laugh out loud.

"Kiera, you saw the last bulletin as did we all. For some reason, one man killed another. I'm not a detective, but I think the French would say '*Cherchez la femme*,' don't you?"

Kiera about drooled at his use of the French. "So romantic."

If Leah rolled her eyes any more, no telling if she'd be able to focus by the time she finished her snack. And my attempt not to laugh came out a snort. And now everyone looked at me.

"Excuse me. I missed the last bulletin, so I may not be up to date. On the news, they said something about drugs? Have they eliminated that possibility since then?"

At least a few of the women turned from him and I noticed his facial expression freeze, his smile no longer friendly. He didn't like losing the attention and I obviously wasn't under his spell.

Leah jumped in. "I heard the same thing, Sheridan. Not much information, but it was looking like it may have been related to drugs. There were some issues here a few years ago, before you arrived, Dr. Antos. Sheridan, you were involved and wasn't the whole drug bust thing related to a murder?"

Not happy she'd brought it up, I didn't have a choice but to answer.

I nodded. "A man was killed in Clover Hill. He was about to close down a drug dealer who used high school and college kids to get other kids hooked and provided the product across the state, including here. Apparently, it was a very lucrative activity, fueled by the dealer's own drug habit and gambling debts. In that case, it was economics and not romance."

Dr. Antos made a big show of looking at his watch and gracefully stood up and stretched, showcasing his trim but muscular physique. With a big smile to most that seemed to disappear when he glanced at me, he commented, "Ladies, the bell is about to ring. Thank you, Claudia, for the delicious treats this morning."

His comment was directed to an older woman and she glowed. He strutted out of the room and there was a collective sigh. I finished my coffee cake, praised the woman who provided it, and left, Leah joining me. She shook her head. "Lunch? In the cafeteria with Mr. Keurig?"

"Sure."

CHAPTER 8

Classes went well and cup in hand, I checked my phone as I walked to the cafeteria. I jumped when someone tapped my shoulder.

"I don't believe we've met. Austin Antos. I teach economics and finance."

"Nice to meet you, Dr. Antos." He was not quite six foot tall. Still his torso was shorter than expected. I resisted the urge to check his shoes to see if he possibly had lifts.

He put his hand up. "Austin, please. To deal with these students and administration, it's best if we are all friends, don't you think?" His mouth turned up but his blue eyes were narrowed, not as shining as earlier.

I nodded. "I'm Sheridan Hendley. I'm a temporary, adjunct faculty in psychology. Part-time. One benefit of my job is steering clear of all the politics."

"Temporary. Adjunct. That explains why I haven't seen you. You would be difficult to forget." His gaze travelled from my face to my feet and back as he spoke. He seemed to think it was a compliment and I wanted to groan.

"Sorry to rush off, but I have a meeting. And I need to call my husband." I smiled and walked away.

In the cafeteria, I grabbed a sandwich and coffee and looked around. Leah stood, waving, and I smiled. We sat a table for four, with only two chairs, in a corner of the large room. Not quiet, but much quieter than the cacophony of voices as I joined her.

"I usually take my lunch back to my office. It's too loud in here."

"In about five minutes, the masses will thin out. Many of them go out to the parking lot and play football as long as it's not too cold. Others gravitate to the library or the computer lab. They can't eat or drink in either. Library is a quiet zone, not so the computer lab."

Even as she spoke, students were exiting. One even slid a chair to our table. I nodded at him. "Thanks."

"Do most of the faculty eat in the teachers' lounge?"

"Not most. The younger crowd tends to gravitate there. Others, like you or me, most times eat in their offices or go to one of the fast-food places or the student center. No leftovers this morning, so here I am."

I smiled. "Was that the younger crowd this morning? Except Claudia, of course."

She nodded. "Definitely. And the gathering was typical of when Austin makes an appearance. Claudia, on the other hand, lives alone and loves to bake. At least once a month, we all reap the benefits."

"I remember once or twice going in there for a quick cup of coffee and seeing cake or cookies. And I recognize her from the library. Were those her goodies?"

"Most likely. Many of us bring in stuff around the holidays – usually cookies, not cake. I walked in with her so I knew it was a good day in the lounge."

"Definitely an interesting dynamic."

She burst out laughing. "One of the reasons, I don't hang out there since Austin joined the faculty. He has his own groupies and they fawn all over him. Most of them are first- or second-year faculty, in their late twenties or early thirties. Not surprisingly, some of them are single. You lucked out not having to be here for the retreat last month. He walked in and the reaction was palpable. One person noticed him and then the next. A chain reaction with everyone watching him. Especially Kiera."

"Let me guess. She teaches literature?"

"Yup, and a fan of everything literary and romantic. She's actually very bright and knowledgeable. I think she's even written a book or two. She's Claudia's niece, by the way."

We had both finished our lunch before Leah spoke again.

"I know how involved you got with that other murder. Isn't this latest one in your old back yard?"

I smiled. "Yes, North Shore is one of the nearest towns. My friends and I would often go there or Alta Vista for something to do."

"Are you involved in the investigation this time? Anything I can do to help?"

"Dr. Addison has made it quite clear that I am not to be involved and to keep Millicent College out of it."

"Ha! All you have to do is look around and know that like any college campus, there's some faction that is involved in drugs. And I don't mean marijuana. I'm friends with Craig Sims at the health center. Based on students showing up wired or not remembering what they did the night before, he suspects someone's dealing here."

I nodded. "It only makes sense that if there was a market for drugs here before, that even when Shane Buchanan's operation was shut down, someone would eventually step in and fill the void. Might not have anything to do with the murder in North Shore, even if it was related to drugs."

"True. I just love a good mystery."

Laughing, I agreed. "The only mystery I need to focus on now is how to wake up my sleepy afternoon class."

We bussed our table and it was back to work. I still needed to let Mrs. Chantilly know I wouldn't be volunteering on Thursday. I'd left a message on voicemail, only she didn't always listen to the messages or track what was said. Brett's last message said he would be home late tonight and we needed to talk. I decided to stop at Pets & Paws on my way home.

Luke and Mrs. Chantilly were both in the kitchen when I walked in. Luke scurried around but didn't say a word. Slim, with white blonde hair, blue eyes, Luke had put on some muscles working at Pets & Paws. At the same time, he'd also lost his attitude. He opened his mouth a few times, shook his head and worked. Mrs. Chantilly, on the other hand, bustled around him, still dressed as a pilgrim.

She paused when she saw me. "Sheridan, it's not the right day. Did you get lost?"

"Not at all. I needed to let you know I won't be in tomorrow. I left you a voicemail."

"I never listen to those things. It would take too much time. Melina should be here any minute. Cookies in the oven."

She turned away and I waited for her to come back, still not sure she understood. Luke walked past me with laundry.

"Luke, do you know if anyone else can volunteer tomorrow? I'm not going to be able to come by."

He stopped and stared. "I… I don't know. Probably not."

"Is everything okay, Luke? How's Cocoa doing?"

His hands stopped fidgeting and he smiled. "She's doing great, much more responsive. Very affectionate. Dr. Barksdale gave her a clean bill of health though she is malnourished."

"I'm so glad to hear it. Tomorrow? I have to go to Cold Creek. I could come by before I leave and take care of the ones that seem the most in need. I feel bad, though."

Mrs. Chantilly joined us. "Here's the next batch of cookies for the dogs. Don't you feel bad, Sheridan. Cocoa is doing good."

She handed me the tray and returned to the kitchen.

Luke shuffled his feet. "I get out early tomorrow, so I'll come in right after school. Susie will be here for the pups and can check on the others."

He reached over and took the tray from me. His expression was pained and the tray shook slightly in his hands. I was about to ask if everything was okay when the door behind me opened.

"Hey, Sheridan. What are you doing here on a Wednesday?"

"Good to see you, Melina. I'm going to Cold Creek tomorrow so I won't be able to help out here. I wanted to let Mrs. Chantilly and Luke know."

"I saw the news. Did you know the man who was killed?"

"No, not at all. But some of my friends there did. Seemed like a good time to visit."

She laughed. "Yeah, a murder and possible drug connection is always a good time to visit if you like mysteries."

Luke almost dropped the tray of cookies and I grabbed for it. Some went flying and the three of us collected them off the ground. He mumbled something and disappeared into the back of the house.

"I sure hope he's not sick. He seems a little off today."

"He does. Maybe he's just tired. I am glad I ran into you though. The visit to Cold Creek? I'm not sure what time I'll be back and Brett is down there, too. Any chance Maddie could go to your house tomorrow?"

"Nedra will be thrilled. And Maddie is no trouble at all. It is a little worrisome that their main topic of conversation is boys. Normal, yet bothersome."

I laughed. "You have that right. I'll let you and Maddie know when we'll get home. I work on Friday, so staying over isn't really an option. Hopefully, this will all blow over so we can check out the foliage over the weekend."

I was running late, nonetheless I made a quick stop in the back to check on Luke. He was nowhere to be found. Odd. I took a few minutes to check on Cocoa and headed home.

CHAPTER 9

Maddie and I arrived home about the same time. She waved, earbuds in, engrossed in conversation, and headed for her room. I let Charlie and Bella out, then in again, and they both trotted toward her room. Dinner would be easy and Brett's last text indicated I had plenty of time to change into more comfy clothes, reheat the pot roast, and make a salad.

A knock on the door interrupted my chopping of vegetables. I was surprised to see Luke when I looked through the peephole and opened the door. He was pale, sweating, and breathing rapidly.

"Luke, are you okay?" I opened the door and he shuffled his feet as he came in.

He took a few deep breaths. "I ... I need to breathe. A minute."

Two things came to mind – drugs or panic attack – and the latter seemed most likely given his comment.

"Have a seat. I'll get you some water."

Always interested in visitors, Charlie and Bella joined us. Charlie settled down on his feet. Bella placed her head in his lap. His hands and eyes instinctively went to her and his posture began to relax, his breathing more even.

"Hi. I remember you. You were the runt of the litter. Maddie got lucky with you. You're beautiful."

Maddie had wandered in and as we watched the change in his demeanor, we both smiled.

"Hi, Luke. You're right. Bella is the best dog, next to Charlie that is."

Luke nodded and leaned so he could give Charlie some affection as well. Then, with a glance at Maddie, he looked at me.

"Sorry for showing up like this. Sorry … I need to talk to Detective McMann. It's important."

"He's not home yet. Best guess is he and Detective Fabry will be here in about 30 minutes. You're welcome to wait. Or I can have him call you. Will your parents be worried if you're not home?"

He shook his head and took a deep breath. "No. Most of the time I'm at Pets & Paws. They'll assume that's where I am." He ran his hand down Bella's back and smiled.

"Then hang out right here. I'll just finish my salad and you can entertain Bella and Charlie."

He nodded. Maddie looked at me and I shrugged. She shrugged back and disappeared. It wasn't up to her to entertain him and he looked quite content with the two dogs giving him comfort and distraction. As much as I wanted to warn Brett, I couldn't figure out how to do that without being too obvious. A glance out the window at Luke's motorcycle assured me Brett would figure it out before he walked in the door.

I finished the salad and set the table, occasionally glancing at Luke and the dogs. He was all tangled up in them and they were eating up the attention and affection. I thought back to the cocky, rude, and arrogant young man he had been when we first met him. And the person who had worked endlessly when the shelter took in more dogs than possible. He'd shown leadership and responsibility then. Now, he seemed fearful and nervous. Something was definitely wrong.

"Luke, can I get you anything?"

"No, ma'am. Thank you. The dogs are the best. How old is Charlie now?"

"She's almost twelve. Getting on in years, but Vanna – Dr. Barksdale – says she's doing good. She seems to have more energy with Bella around."

He nodded. "I've thought about maybe being a vet or a vet tech like Susie. Dogs are much better than humans most of the time. I'm not so sure about cats or other animals though."

I chuckled. "Dogs are definitely more loyal and loving than many humans. I'm not a cat person myself so I don't know about them."

We both heard the garage door and the dogs abandoned him as they bounded to the door to greet the new arrivals. When it took more than a minute, Bella returned to Luke. He had stiffened up with their arrival, and Bella seemed to sense it. Maybe she would make a good therapy dog.

Brett and Fabry walked in. A quick kiss and Brett commented, "Fabry, you know where the bathroom is by now."

Fabry nodded to Brett and then to Luke, and headed down the hall. Brett turned back to me. "Have the dogs been out? Time for a little Frisbee?"

"No, not in the past hour, anyway. And yes, there's time for Frisbee."

"Luke, how about you give me a hand?"

"I can do that. I…"

"Then let's go. Come on Charlie, Bella. Play time."

Luke followed Brett out the door with the dogs. I was marveling at my husband's perception, when Maddie whispered, "I hope it was okay. I texted Dad that Luke was here, upset, and wanted to talk to him."

I smiled and gave her a hug. My husband was still a marvel, if not clairvoyant, and so was his daughter.

Fabry joined us and looked around.

"They're outside with the dogs."

He nodded and sat down. "Tell me about Max. Brett turns various shades of red when his name comes up. Did you date him or something?"

Maddie giggled. I laughed so hard, my eyes teared. "No, I never dated Max. Have you met Max, yet?"

"No. I only saw him in the distance. Tomorrow is the day. I just want to be prepared. Hirsch keeps needling Brett about him and Brett gets all red in the face and shakes his head."

"Ever seen a meme of the absent-minded professor? Hair sticking out every which way? Trying for the put together look in a suit, only his shirt is buttoned wrong? Shouting about how important his research is, but his mice have escaped? The first time they met, Brett asked to have a few words with him, and Max told Brett he was too busy for him."

I couldn't help it. I laughed so hard I couldn't stop. Maddie, too. Even Fabry had to chuckle at my description.

As I was about to expound further on Max, the back door opened. Brett and Luke walked in, Brett's arm around Luke's shoulders, the dogs almost tripping the two of them.

"Looks like we missed something pretty funny."

"Sheridan was describing Dr. Max to Uncle James."

Brett shook his head, his face flushing. "Please. Let me enjoy dinner. It smells delicious and I'm starving." He turned to Luke. "I believe there's a place set for you. Will you join us?"

Luke nodded and took the chair Brett had indicated. Maddie and Brett helped me get everything on the table. Conversation at the table was stilted until I realized I'd hadn't told Maddie about the trip to Cold Creek.

"Maddie, Kim called yesterday and things are a little crazy in Cold Creek. That's why Fabry asked about Max. I'm going to go down there tomorrow and visit with Kim for sure. Probably Max, too. He called as well. I'll definitely be back though I'm not sure when. Melina said it would be okay for you to go home with Nedra."

She smiled. "I know. Nedra told me. We're all set."

"Good, glad to hear it." I felt bad she'd found out from Nedra, though, not from me. With Luke showing up, there hadn't been a chance.

Another lull.

"Any idea what the weather is supposed to be this weekend? Have you heard when the foliage is supposed to peak here?"

Brett smiled. "Maddie, did you look up the foliage information yet?"

She nodded. "Yup. It's already peaking in New England. The pictures of Vermont were beautiful. Already started here and south. Maybe this weekend or next will peak. To go hiking, one of the next two weekends would be good. Most likely, the second one."

"Great. We'll have to make some plans then." Brett leaned back in his chair. "That was delicious, Sher."

"Definitely. Best part of partnering with Brett is the food. And the company of you and Maddie, of course." We all laughed.

"It was delicious, Ms. Hendley. Better than Mrs. Chantilly's for sure."

Maddie's hand flew to her mouth.

"Oh my gosh, you don't eat those cookies she bakes, do you?"

Luke laughed. The first time I'd seen him laugh in a long time I realized.

"She cooks regular meals sometimes. I think only if I'm working late.." His voice dropped and he mumbled, "Or she's expecting company."

He stood. No one ever discussed that her company was in the form of Blake Buchanan, past mayor of Clover Hill and Luke's grandfather.

"Anyway, thank you for everything. I didn't mean to barge in. And the food was great."

"No dessert?"

He shook his head. "Thanks, but no."

Brett stood. "I'll walk you out, Luke."

"My hint was ignored. Luke may not want dessert, but I sure do."

"Fabry, I know you want dessert. You always do. Apple pie, heated, with a scoop of ice cream?"

He nodded as did Maddie. "Four plates, all the same, coming up. Maddie give me a hand with the ice cream, please."

CHAPTER 10

By the time dessert was served, Brett came back in. He took charge of coffee and we all waited. Fortunately, we didn't have to wait long.

"This is great." Brett cleared his throat. "Maddie, are you aware of or heard of any talk about designer drugs at the high school?"

She grimaced. "I'm not sure. What exactly are 'designer drugs' anyway?"

"Sometimes, they're called 'club drugs' instead. Some examples are ecstasy or Molly. Another one is rohypnol or Roofies. They're drugs that are manufactured illegally. They include things other than what was intended to boost effects and they can be dangerous."

"Different from cocaine or heroin or opioids?"

"Yes. And no. Those are also illegal and bad news, and addictive. Cocaine is sometimes added to the ecstasy as a boost. Designer drugs are very dangerous, often lethal. And marketed often to teens. The capsules may have comics or flowers on them."

Fabry added, "Another 'fun' activity is taking drugs from their parents – prescribed, legal drugs – and mixing them to create something that is dangerous and no one really knows what the effect may be. Whatever they call it, the result is dangerous and often ends in death."

Maddie nodded. "I haven't heard anyone talk about those specific drugs. Well, actually in one of our health classes last year, someone came and talked to us about Roofies. Warned everyone to be careful of leaving any drinks, even juice or soda, unattended at a party."

"Maddie, did they tell you why they came to school then?"

She shook her head.

Brett explained. "At one of the schools, out of state, there was an incident. A middle school party at the school had big bowls of punch. They'd mixed some fruit punch with some ginger ale and ice cream. Pretty standard fare. Even with all the chaperones, someone had spiked the punch with Rohypnol. Used to be someone would try adding alcohol. Pouring something into a punch bowl is a lot more obvious than some powder in your hand as you stir the punch. Several students felt the effects and at least one passed out, while still at the dance."

Maddie's mouth dropped. "That's awful. Wait, what does that have to do with Luke?"

"Nothing."

When all three of us stared at him, he shook his head.

"Nothing so far as his dealing or taking or anything. He heard talk and is worried about it. For the risks and because Roofies in particular were mentioned in relation to a party. Someone came up to him and asked where to find them. He's worked so hard and yet, he feels he still has the 'bad boy' image among at least some of his peers. He's very afraid that he'll be accused or give in or end up like Caleb."

"What about Caleb?" Caleb Buchanan was Luke's cousin and was on partial release from the rehabilitation center after dealing with his opioid addiction.

"As far as Luke knows, Caleb is holding his own. His parents have him on a pretty tight leash and he sees a counselor weekly with required drug testing."

"Sher, did you tell Dad what Luke was like when he showed up?"

"No chance. When I saw Luke at Pets & Paws, he was visibly nervous, shaken by something. When he got here? He was having a panic attack. I'm surprised he hadn't crashed the bike on his way."

Brett nodded. "He told me. He said he had them for a while right after the situation with his uncle's murder and getting arrested and all. They only started again after someone asked him about drugs. Now, anytime someone tries for a private conversation, he panics. He's afraid to go to the bathroom as that's where a lot of the talk goes on."

"What will happen next? How can we help him?"

"I'll have a chat with local police, call Peabody tonight. Hopefully, they can get someone into the high school undercover and ferret the source or sources out. That and see that the high school has an assembly or somehow gets the word out about Roofies."

"And Luke?" Maddie asked.

Brett shrugged. "What's worked so far is getting positive feedback when he does good. And the dogs. And hope it all works out."

Maddie nodded. "Okay. I have to get homework done." She picked up her dishes and ours and stuck them in the sink. "Later."

We busied ourselves cleaning up and getting food put away, though Fabry decided the last piece of pie looked lonely.

"Luke aside, what's the status on the murder and Max?"

James nodded to Brett. "I'm eating. You talk."

"Landry is best described as an entrepreneur. Real estate, commercial expansion, some urban planning. He's the one who figured out the properties to buy and the franchises that would work in North Shore, help to put it on the map so to speak. Leavitt's Brew Pub and the Egg Spot, for example. He has some other businesses ready to launch."

"Could his murder be business-related?"

"I don't think so. This murder feels more drug-related than business or personal, partly because of where it was. Business or domestic issues aren't usually settled in the woods. Then again, if a hot head is after someone, they might follow a person to a campsite."

"Why drug-related?"

"Landry was known to be involved in the past, both as a user and a dealer of designer drugs. And, the initial tox screen was positive. For Roofies."

"Huh? The person who shot him wanted to be sure he didn't fight back?"

"That's the best theory we have so far. Subdue him, shoot him, leave him in the woods to bleed out. And that implies that the killer had access to the drugs."

"How does this involve Max then? He has no history of drug involvement."

"No, he doesn't. In his ranting about the dog poop and Landry coming by his house a lot, Max accused Landry of flirting with Stella. Neighbors heard him ask Landry why he was flirting with Stella and heard him threaten Landry."

James pushed his plate away. "If in fact he was honing in on Stella, was he going to try to liven up her dreary existence with drugs or was he going to drug her and rape her. Either way, Landry is a risk to Stella. Max threatened Landry and that gives him a motive."

"We got the warrants to search Max's office and lab tonight. We start there at 8 o'clock. The warrant for his home should be signed by the time we finish with his office and lab."

"And you're looking for what?"

"The gun or drugs or both. It's not likely we'll find anything, yet we have to do due diligence. Max definitely has a temper."

"Oh, and we get to question both Max and Stella separately." He groaned. "I'm hoping you can occupy him while we do the office search, maybe get him calmed down. My thought is that Detective Fabry will do his interview."

Fabry shook his head. "So, Sheridan, anything else I should know about your friend Max?"

"He's prone to hysteria and tirades about his rights? And you should both know, Joe has already been bothering him and asking him questions and generally getting him excited and scared."

CHAPTER 11

Up early, I was surprised to see Maddie in the kitchen, making cookies of all things. Peanut butter cookies.

"You're up early and baking? What's up?"

"Luke's been working so hard. He needs some reinforcement. After school, Ms. Melina is taking Nedra and me to Pets & Paws, and we'll bring Luke some cookies for all his hard work."

"That's very nice of you, Maddie."

She shrugged. "He doesn't seem to have family that support him. Only Mrs. Chantilly and, well, she's …she's different. It doesn't seem like his parents or even his grandfather, Mr. Buchanan, interact with him much. Least not when we see them both at Pets & Paws."

I nodded. She was right on. Blake Buchanan didn't exactly act grandfatherly or interact with Luke much when he visited the shelter. It was pretty obvious Blake was watching over Mrs. Chantilly. And the nuances of their relationship had to be awkward for Luke, given the family ties.

"That's a good thought and a not quite so random act of kindness you're doing. I'm sure he'll appreciate it. Just be sure you clean up the mess."

She nodded and worked on it as she moved trays in and out of the oven. Most of the area clean, she squealed, "I'm late!" and bolted to her room. I packed up the cookies, leaving a dozen for the house. And set aside a couple to enjoy with my coffee.

Frantic, Maddie ran into the kitchen and stopped short as I handed her the container of cookies.

"Here ya go. Behave for Ms. Melina. I'll call when we figure out what time we'll be home."

She nodded, took the cookies, and dashed out the door. The house was quiet. Fabry had picked up Brett even before I was awake. I took a deep breath, ate my cookies, and got ready to go.

Looking at the clock, I muttered to myself, "They're probably already in his office" and chuckled. Max's office, like everything else related to Max, most often looked like a typhoon had gone through and upended everything.

About half way to Cold Creek, Brett's text showed up on the screen, "Terra or Ali notified Max. He's on his way in. What's your ETA?"

I dictated my response "Thirty minutes or so."

As I had guessed, Max and I arrived at the college about the same time. He almost knocked me over as I walked out of Georg's café coffee in hand.

"Careful, Max. How are you?"

"Sheridan, I don't understand what's going on. Terra called me and said the police were searching my office, had a search warrant. What do they think I could possibly have that's connected to Landry's death?"

"Max, you need to chill, here. It's not a question of what are they looking for. Is there anything in your office the police shouldn't see?"

"My results. The mice experiments. That's all proprietary information – intellectual property."

"They're too busy to read papers and nothing in the papers is related to Mr. Landry's death, right?" I hesitated and asked, "Max, in your experiments with the mice, were you ever testing drug effects?"

"What? No, I study learning and behavioral response. Food if you go down this path, mild shock if you go down that path. The only time drugs were ever in the lab was when someone from the vet clinic came in and euthanized the mice. All because that stupid man closed my lab. He had no sense of science or research."

He ranted on about the Chancellor and President of Cold Creek College and how they didn't value research. They closed down his research and refused to endorse his writing any more grants, arguing that for a private four-year-college, he was wasting a lot of money. Of course, the trigger for this had nothing to do with money, but politics.

We reached the Psychology Department offices and Terra and Ali waved, eyes wide as they spotted not only me but Max. Administrative assistants for the department, they kept everything going smoothly, most of the time. Terra, the more outgoing of the two, walked toward us.

"You have to stop them, Terra. That is my office and my work. Why haven't you stopped them?"

"Dr. Bentley, calm down. We can't stop them. They have a warrant to search your office and your lab. Detective Fabry suggested you might want to call your lawyer if you're concerned."

She hesitated briefly, but continued as he started to walk toward his office. "Dr. Bentley, you can wait in the departmental office or you can sit in my office. You aren't allowed near or in your office while they search."

"What? I have to be sure they don't steal anything or move anything out of place, mess with my system."

I snorted, trying hard not to laugh. "Sorry. Max is there anything valuable in your office or lab?"

"My research is valuable, Sheridan. You just never understood. Dr. Grant never understood. No one here understands the value of research." Arms waving, his voice got louder and louder. Students peaked around the corners and I heard doors opening and closing.

"Max, try to stay calm. We can sit and chat and you can tell me about Stella and your new house." I gasped as I said house, realizing he still didn't know that was part of the plan.

"Sheridan, you need to make your husband stop. Can you do that for me? I've been a good friend to you, helped you out."

"Max, I don't think you murdered that man. I don't think anyone really thinks you did. They have to check out every lead."

"And it's Detective Fabry, not Brett in your office." Terra added. She looked at me and pointed down. I smiled. Brett was in the lab downstairs.

"So how about it, Max? Sit and bring me up to date on all that's happening in your life until they're done with your office."

He nodded and Terra volunteered her office. As we settled in, I asked Terra to let Kim know where we were. I had no doubt she'd tell more people than Kim. My only hope was that Max would calm down before Fabry showed up to interview him or he got the call from Stella they were at the house. He was flushed and sweating, his hands shaking as we settled into the chairs in Terra's office.

"Tell me about your new house. What prompted you to move out of Cold Creek?"

"Stella's mom passed and left her some money. She was heartbroken and her mother's will said something about using the money to invest in real estate. Stella checked on properties we could buy to rent, all in Cold Creek. I never knew so many people rented."

A small four-year private school, students lived in the dorms at least for the first two years or commuted from home. It never occurred to me their homes were rentals either.

"Who is renting – not specifically, but generally? Students?"

"Some students, yes. No available apartments and what the realtor said was some of them want to be on their own so three or four rent a house. Sheridan, some faculty members rent instead of own. I didn't know that either. Especially, new faculty. It was an eye-opener for me."

"And you decided?"

"The realtor convinced us – this is all her fault – that we should look to buy a bigger house and rent our small one. She's the one who found the house in North Shore. It's this new development of larger houses and all tucked into the woods. It's not in the town itself, about a fifteen-minute drive to the new coffee shop there. And bigger than our other house. And… and Sheridan? It wasn't as expensive as buying one the same size in Cold Creek."

That sounded odd. "Stella likes the house?"

"She picked it out and was emphatic about one thing."

Stella tended to not speak up much and followed Max's lead most times. His statement intrigued me.

"Emphatic about what?"

"There's a room downstairs that could be a master bedroom or study, with its own bath. All wheel-chair accessible." He shook his head. "When her mother was dying, Stella wanted to bring her here to Cold Creek. We didn't have room. She was emphatic that whatever we bought had the space and could accommodate either of my parents if needed."

I smiled and patted his arm. "That was very sweet of her."

We chatted about other topics for a while. I kept glancing at my watch waiting for the next trigger to Max's hysteria.

CHAPTER 12

As voices reached us, we both turned to the opening door. I recognized Joe's voice before he strutted in. Max visibly tensed and his coffee sloshed over the top as he set it down, not too gently. I patted Max's arm again as I stood and intercepted Joe.

"Hi, Joe. Good to see you. I hope we have a chance to chat while I'm in town."

He gave me the acceptable side hug. "We were just saying you needed to be here. Murder and you seem to go together. I need to interview Max."

A grunt from behind me made me smile. "I don't think so, Joe. Not right now. We're having a private conversation and Max told me he doesn't want to talk to you. That right, Max?"

"Absolutely. I don't want to talk to him."

"Now look, the press and the public have a right to hear your side of the story, Max. This is your chance to talk about your relationship with Landry and clear your name."

I arched my eyebrow and scowled at Joe as Max grunted behind me. "Sorry, Joe. You need to get your information from official sources. I think Terra explained that Chief Hirsch and Detective Fabry are here right now. I'm sure they will have a statement for you later today. I'm also sure they will clear Max of any wrong-doing, aren't you?"

Joe shuffled his feet and with a nudge I prompted him to leave the office. I used tissues to clean up the spilled the coffee. Before I could engage Max in conversation, increasingly loud voices drew near. I recognized Fabry's and Hirsch's voices in the mix.

"Thank you, Sheridan, for making him go away. He's like a blood hound and after my blood." His voice was low and unsteady. "I just don't know what to do. I didn't kill anyone. I can't even kill spiders. And Landry was a big guy, even bigger than Brett."

I nodded and turned as the door opened. Fabry cleared his voice and took a step into the office, Hirsch behind him.

"Dr. Bentley, Dr. Hendley. Good morning. Dr. Bentley, this is Detective Fabry. We need to talk to you about Mr. Landry. We can do that here or at the police station. What's your preference?"

I watched as Max's mouth opened and closed and nothing came out. "Max, you need to talk to them, okay. Do you want to do that here? Or go to the station?"

"Here." His voice squeaked. I stood up and disposed of my now empty coffee cup.

"You're leaving?"

"Yes, Max. They need to talk to you and it's getting crowded in here. I'm not going far. Getting another cup of coffee and then I'll probably be in Kim's office."

Both men nodded to me as I stepped out and pulled Terra's door shut firmly. I shooed Terra, Joe, and Ali away from the area. With a glance back at the door, I headed to Kim's office. Hugs exchanged we went downstairs to Georg's, got three coffees and made our way to Max's lab.

To anyone who didn't know better, the immediate reaction to the mess with police and dogs would be to blame them. Kim and I laughed as we watched one of the men in a police vest straighten a pile of papers as he retrieved them from the floor. Max's lab might look better when they were finished.

The man closest to us walked in our direction. He was older and portly.

"Sorry, ladies. Police business. Please be on your way."

"Officer, is Detective McMann available?"

His gaze narrowed and he spoke into his collar mic. "McMann still here? Someone at the door wants him."

His face softened a little. "Yes, that's correct." After a short pause, "I'll tell her."

"Mrs. McMann?"

I nodded and he continued. "He'll be right here, but you both need to stay in the hall."

"That's fine. Thank you."

He eyed the two coffees in my hands, and loathe as I was to give up a cup of coffee, I was polite. "Coffee – regular?"

"Nah. But thanks. Appreciate the gesture." He walked away and Kim and I stepped back from the door.

"How was Max holding up?"

"Obstinate and hysterical, as usual. He didn't seem to understand his lab was being searched as well as his office and at least Fabry and Hirsch are doing the interview. They're concerned with murder and he's talking about intellectual property. Geesh. I hope he didn't think Landry was going to steal his mice data."

Kim chuckled. "His data are useless. What I don't get? Administration closed his lab – this lab – a year ago. Why hasn't it been cleaned out and re-purposed yet?"

I shrugged. "Maybe they haven't figured out a new purpose. Any ideas?"

The lab space was filled with lab tables, cages, and lots of equipment. Even with that, it could accommodate twenty students working on different things. In reality, Max only had one or two, maybe three, students at any one time. Not good use of the space. The room was fitted for what he needed, with running water, sinks, and so on. To convert it to a single classroom would not make sense. A small college, classes generally capped at twenty students and senior seminars were only ten to twelve.

"Two possibilities. One would be to turn this into a computer lab. Yes, there's already one in another building, but this would be more convenient for students in this building. And see if someone in science can use any of this equipment. The second would be to convert this to two rooms – one a classroom and one a true student lounge with charging stations for phones and tablets and laptops."

I nodded and then smiled as Brett walked toward us. He side-hugged Kim and gave me a hug and kiss, wary of the coffee cups.

"Here you go. A mess, huh?"

"That is an understatement. And the garbage hadn't been emptied in who knows how long. The place stunk when we opened it up. Thankfully, there is a back door. Did you know that?"

Kim and I both shook our heads.

"Anyway, the first thing we did was open the door, remove the garbage, and get the fans going. Which, of course, added to the loose paper on the floor." He shook his head.

"Where does the back door go?"

"To the dumpster out back."

"He always kept everything locked up tight, if not orderly."

"And the door was bolted and locked from the inside."

"Have you found anything? Dogs find anything?"

"Lots and lots of paper. No offense, but the amount of paper he went through represents a lot of trees. Didn't he take what he needed when they closed the lab?"

Kim nodded. "He had to come down, deal with any remaining mice, disassemble his mazes and other equipment. The latter are all in storage. He was told to clean out anything he wanted and he turned in the key."

"Kim had just mentioned that nothing's been done since then."

Brett pulled his fingers through his dark curly hair and shook his head. "Anything dated is more than a year old. We're about done and as soon as Fabry and Hirsch finish with him, we'll be heading to the house."

"I'd gotten him calmed down – well, as calm as he ever is – and then Joe showed up, followed by Fabry and Hirsch."

Brett nodded. "They didn't find anything either. I truly feel bad for Max, but he made a threat and the man he threatened is dead."

CHAPTER 13

Fabry and Hirsch came down to the lab when they finished the interview. Next stop was the house, and I went with Fabry to help keep Max and Stella occupied. The new house was easily twice the size of their previous home. What had been crowded in their old home barely filled this one. Two stories, with the master suite on one end of the first floor. The most amazing thing about the house and yard was that they were immaculate. Nothing out of place.

We were told to make ourselves comfortable in the patio. They allowed us to take coffee with us, though Stella had tea instead. The tension was high and I tried to make conversation.

"This is a beautiful area and you've done a great job with the house and yard. How do you like living so far out, Stella?"

"It's very peaceful. If I need anything, I can hop in the car and be in the center of town in less than 15 minutes. And North Shore is growing. The new community center has a lot of activities, and I've gotten involved in some of them. Sometimes, there are noises in the woods around us. They bother me, but Max tells me it's just the wild life. I think I saw a fox once and spotted a few deer."

"Is there a neighborhood watch or listserv to alert you to anything like the fox or traffic issues or weather?"

Stella grimaced and I continued, "We're on a listserv in Clover Hill. We get notices of lost pets, found pets, and all sorts of stuff. Most of the time I don't read the posts unless it's about a lost dog or pet."

Neither said a word so I waited. Max finally spouted, "No watch, no listserv, but some nosy neighbors."

"I only noticed one other house close to here."

Max stood and walked to the edge of the patio. Stella looked at him and then answered.

"It is a new neighborhood. Moss Builders bought up land and they built about six houses so far. This is one of the smaller ones. You must have missed a couple of them. The side roads are hidden by trees. The nearest neighbor is through the trees over there." She pointed to where Max was standing.

"That's where Landry lived. His wife, Celeste … I heard she left him a couple months ago. On the other side, about the same distance are the Hortons. He's in construction and works for Moss Builders. She's a teacher. They have four children."

I don't know if she would have kept talking about the neighbors. Hirsch came to the patio door and interrupted.

"Dr. Bentley, there's a package you need to sign for. I'll walk you through the house."

"Package? I'm not expecting a package. Stella, did you order something?"

She shook her head. "I'm not expecting a package either."

Hirsch shrugged. "Let's all go to the front of the house and straighten this out."

We followed him through the house and out the front door. The driver handed Max a clipboard with one hand, a package in the other.

"Where is the package from? We didn't order anything."

The driver looked around and shrugged. "I'm sorry if this is inconvenient. My job is to deliver this package to this address for Connor Landry. Just sign, so I can go…"

Hirsch lunged for the package and jerked it away from the driver. At the same time, one of the leashed police dogs pulled at his handler's grasp.

"Hirsch? Package."

Hirsch moved closer and the dog's reaction heightened. Hirsch put the package on the ground and, once unleashed, the dog immediately went into guard position at the package. Hirsch turned to the driver.

"Paperwork and license, please."

Hirsch reviewed the paperwork, took a picture of the paperwork and the driver's license, then handed them back to the driver.

"Wait! I need someone to sign for that package. Attest that I did my job in delivering it."

Hirsch took the clipboard back, wrote something on the paperwork, and gave it back to him. The driver couldn't get out of there fast enough.

The handler called the dog off and Hirsch retrieved the package, nodding. He looked to Max and Stella.

"Do you often get packages that are addressed to Landry or his wife, or anyone named Cabot or Jarvit, but with this address?"

Max shook his head.

Stella whispered, "Once before. Two weeks ago. It didn't need a signature and was left on the step. I walked over with it and no one was home at the Landry's. I left it on their step."

Hirsch nodded.

"You did what? You went to his house?" Max was flailing his arms and I grabbed one before it hit me. Stella's eyes were wide.

"Calm down, Max."

Hirsch shook his head, but Max shut up. "Okay, back to the patio. Let's get that package secured and finish up here. These people would like their lives back."

We were escorted back to the patio and waited. We sat on the patio and looked out over lush greenery, the blue sky above. Nobody wanted to talk and we all pulled out our phones. I had several messages from Brett, Kim, and even Marty.

"Max? I think you'll be in the clear after this. If not, Marty Cohn – the attorney who represented Zoe from the Grill – texted me to say he's happy to meet with you if you need legal counsel."

It was like all his energy evaporated. His face fell, his shoulders slouched.

"Thank you. I can't take much more. Send me his information, please. I sure hope I don't need it."

A few clicks later I said, "Done."

Behind us, Hirsch cleared his throat. "We're done as well. You can have your house and office back. Detective Fabry and I need to have a conversation with Stella and then we will be out of your hair."

"Come on, Max. Let's go inside and you can show me the house while they talk to Stella and enjoy some fresh air."

He hesitated until Stella said, "Go along. I'll be okay."

By the time we finished the upstairs and came back down, the dogs and handlers were nowhere to be seen. Only Hirsch.

"We're done here. We tried not to make a mess. Sheridan, I'll give you a ride back to Cold Creek."

I nodded. After hugs to Max and Stella, I left with Hirsch.

"Fabry went to the Landry home. He and Brett will meet us at the Grill with any updates."

"And the package?"

"On its way to the lab to determine what the contents are."

CHAPTER 14

Zoe immediately hugged me when we entered the Grill. It hadn't changed much. Smiling as she was, she looked younger than the last time we'd visited.

"Zoe, it's great to see you. You look great."

She nodded and beamed. "Thank you. I wish you could see Rebekah. She's doing well in college. But, let's get you and Chief Hirsch some coffee. Will Brett be joining you?" Her eyebrows arched.

"Yes, he will."

She seated us and served our coffees, not waiting for the waitstaff to take care of us. "We figured with a murder near here, you would be coming to town. No offense to Chief Hirsch, but somehow you always were better at unraveling what was really going on. Even at your own risk."

Hirsch started to say something and shook his head as Fabry joined us.

"Zoe, I'm just glad that everything has turned out well for you and Rebekah, and the rest of your family. And, of course, for the Grill. Cold Creek wouldn't be the same without this place."

With a shake of her head, she whispered. "There've been rumors, you know…"

Hirsch leaned forward. "Zoe, can you share those rumors with us? May be important."

"I hate to even say this out loud, you know. That Landry fellow?"

We all nodded in anticipation and Fabry sat up straight.

"He said something about getting a new franchise here for a barbecue place and a Starbucks and an Eggspot like they opened in North Shore. Can you believe that? Or all the building going on up there in North Shore?"

Fabry deflated and I struggled not to laugh. Hirsch tried for more information.

"Zoe, sooner or later, those things will probably happen. What else do you know about Landry? Does he come here often?"

She shrugged. "Often enough, and he's always talking about needing more choices in Cold Creek. And sometimes he's with that Skinner guy. You remember him? He was involved in that boy's murder a few years back. He must have gotten some kind of deal to be out so fast."

I nodded. "Have you seen Skinner around other than with Landry?"

"Some other man. Same age, balding, and shorter. Landry? He's a big guy. The other one not so much. Not as friendly or talkative either, though I saw him talking to Mrs. Landry. I never heard his name."

She shook her head and turned as the bell on the door signaled another customer and Brett. She rushed off to get more coffee. Brett joined us and soon had a fresh cup of coffee. Zoe hovered and we quickly placed our orders.

"Zoe was just telling us about Landry's plans for Cold Creek, and about seeing Jared Skinner, and some other man. And Mrs. Landry."

"Mrs. Landry come here often?" Brett asked after a sip of coffee.

"The two of them – Mr. and Mrs. Landry – they'd come in for lunch every once in a while. Come to think of it, not lately though. Occasionally, she'd come in alone. From her clothes, they obviously have money." She took our order and then disappeared.

I turned to the three men. "Well?"

"Interesting morning, but other than pretty much eliminating Max as a suspect – absolutely no evidence to support his involvement – not very productive." Brett shook his head and slouched.

"Oh, but it was productive in some ways." Fabry's comment had Brett sitting up and glancing from Fabry to me with wide eyes.

"Not about Max, Brett. At least I don't think so."

Fabry chuckled. "Absolutely not about Max. Though we, Hirsch actually, intercepted a package delivered to Max's house, but addressed to Connor

Landry. Text I just got confirmed what the canine assigned to us sensed. Drugs. Designer drugs. That puts Landry involved with the drugs, possibly Cabot and Jarvit, too."

"Why the wrong address? Honestly, I don't see Max as a drug user or dealer. My opinion aside, couldn't Cabot, Jarvit, and Landry argue the drugs weren't theirs and claim that Max or Stella used his name to cover up their connection?"

Fabry smiled. "The driver went to the wrong house. Twice, apparently. The address was Cabot's only Max's house is easier to see and the same street. And no number on either house. No one was home when I stopped there. Tally was working on the search warrant and on locating Mrs. Landry."

"Anything else new?" Hirsch asked.

"Landry? They're still working on the rest of the drug screen. Positive for opioids and other drugs. I'm surprised the combination with the Roofies didn't kill him."

Fabry broke into a smile and his eyes twinkled as Zoe returned. Conversation stalled for a bit until Fabry glanced at his phone again. "Eat fast. They're working on the search warrants as we feast." With that he dug in as if he hadn't eaten in weeks.

"How was Max holding up?" Brett asked before he attacked his lunch.

"Okay, all things considered. He calmed down at the college, until Joe showed up. He was worried that you would read his notes and steal his research... his world was being violated and he had no control. Not good feelings."

Brett hesitated, his sandwich halfway to his mouth. "Probably how many people feel, those who are innocent at least. How was Stella?"

"Surprisingly calm. And she's the one who found the first package and delivered it to Landry's house. She said he and his wife split? Have you talked to her, or Jarvit and Cabot?"

Both men shrugged. "Not other than as witnesses to help establish a time frame for Landry's whereabouts. We didn't pay much attention to Jarvit. Or Cabot, for that matter."

"We may need to revisit our notes, Brett. If Cabot was the one who verified or refuted and not Jarvit, we may need to talk to Jarvit again and vice versa."

"And with a little more direct questions about designer drugs. There was a drug operation here previously that involved Skinner. He may be a place to start, especially if Cabot and Jarvit don't know we've made a connection."

"Back then, didn't you find connections across the state?" I'd been so concerned with exonerating the groundskeeper, I hadn't paid much attention beyond finding the murderer.

"Yup. We were able to trace the connections across the state. As is often the case, the center was closer to a major city. In this case running from Roanoke to Richmond and extending north. Like the situation in Clover Hill with the Buchanans. That was more the opioids though.

"Couldn't the same people or the same connections be used for both?" It seemed like a logical conclusion to me.

"Not likely the same people behind both at a local level. Tend to be more specialized. Could a larger operation have different routes for different drugs? Certainly. But the 'marketing' or pull for the drugs is different. Opioids make the pain go away, while designer drugs are all about taking risks, getting the ride of your life. Or, in the case of Roofies, ensuring the person has no control. Different motivation, different market, different seller and dealer, at least at the local level. The fact that sometimes cocaine is mixed in, like in ecstasy, suggests ready access though – up the chain, all drugs are likely."

Fabry nodded in agreement. "We definitely need to lean on Skinner and follow his contacts to the next contact, and so on. Follow all the threads as far as we can. There's been talk that some of the drug business was extending into vaping, a legal means for medical marijuana in some states and a better means for ingesting the drug than smoking. Unfortunately, there's nothing to stop those in production from coming up with vape products for other illegal drugs. There have been some indications that this is already happening. Very scary."

"On the other hand, with accidental deaths associated with vaping, the regulations on vaping have become more restrictive – at least for minors." Hirsch shook his head.

"Wow. That is scary. And I bet easier to do in plain sight. Certainly, vaping the marijuana doesn't give off the same sweet smell of smoking it. But there are limits on which drugs can be converted for vaping, right?

"As far as we know, Sheridan, but the unknown?" Fabry shrugged and I realized he tended to be more cynical and negative than Brett.

A beep on all their phones ended our discussion and my education on vaping. Brett handed me my keys.

"Warrant is done and they've located Mrs. Landry. We're meeting Tally at Landry's house and then we'll go from there. Let me know when you decide to head back to Clover Hill."

We all stood and with a quick kiss from Brett as he handed me my keys, the three men left. As they walked out the door, Zoe looked at me, the bill in her hand. I got the check.

CHAPTER 15

I left the Grill and strolled down the main street of Cold Creek. Quaint shops and memories of my years here. Some good and some bad. There was still only one dentist, Wayne, and I knew from Kim he was still single and as boring as ever. A wave of nostalgia swept over me as I walked down the street without recognizing some of the stores or people.

Turning to find my car, I realized I hadn't talked to Mitch much since our wedding. He'd taken over the counseling center on campus. Kim was teaching until 3 o'clock and I had time to visit if he was around. A quick text and I walked back to the college and the counseling center. No point in fighting for a parking space on campus.

Mitch Pilsner had talked of retiring for years and opening a bed and breakfast. He certainly was of age for retirement, only he hadn't taken that step yet. As a clinical psychologist who did some pro bono work in the community, he'd been a natural for the counseling center. These days, I knew from Kim, he worked only half-time and that was mostly at the counseling center.

I walked in and found the waiting room much warmer and welcoming than I remembered. I let the student worker know who I was and sat down. There were two students waiting as well, their heads down and focused on their tablets.

Mitch came out, smiling and warm. With a hug, he escorted me into the back. "I half expected you to show up, what with a murder and all." He chuckled and rolled his eyes as he added, "Not to mention Max's involvement. Coffee?"

"Your own Keurig? Sure. I got a call from Kim and then one from him. Spent most of the morning with Max and then Max and Stella."

"That serious, huh?" He shook his head. "Max and 'murder' don't even belong in the same sentence. 'Max' and 'hysteria,' more likely."

"You know the process. My impression is that he's no longer a person of interest. Then again, if he spouts off about the victim… He can be his own worst enemy. Enough about Max. How are you and Dora doing? How much longer you going to keep this up?" I waved my arms around his office.

"I think this is the last year. We're both doing well." With a shrug he added, "Some days we both feel our age and we have some travel we want to do while we still can. I've let them know they need to find someone else for next year. You interested?" His eyes twinkled.

"Interested, maybe, but with Maddie's schedule and Brett's schedule? Not practical."

"You're not someone to sit home. What are you doing?"

I laughed. "Staying home and doing nothing but watching for dust to collect lasted only as long as I was still unpacking. Definitely didn't suit me. This is my second year as a visiting faculty member at Millicent College and, when I'm not working, I volunteer at our local dog shelter. So I'm keeping busy."

"After all this time, you must have had a reason for stopping by, besides to catch up. What's up?"

"Just this week, there was some talk about designer drugs in Clover Hill. May or may not be related to the murder here. Any scuttlebutt or rumors related to that here?"

His smile disappeared as I spoke, replaced with a grimace. He nodded. "Not sure why Roofies are lumped in with ecstasy and the hodge-podge homemade combinations. Not sure why, no matter how many ways we tell kids to beware, they don't listen."

He shook his head and continued. "After a party at an undisclosed location, we had a very busy Monday morning. Three juniors came in at different times. All three same story. They went to this party with their friends. They remember having a good time but had no recollection of leaving the party. When they woke up, they were in the arboretum, a good distance from their dorm or rental, and had no idea how they got there."

"Anything else?"

"A quick trip to the emergency room was the next stop for each of them. I don't know what the outcome was. They didn't come back here.

"Awful. Horrific. Did they give any names of others at the party? Police investigating?"

"Didn't amount to anything. They checked with the guys at the rental house. Hirsch said the boys confirmed a party. None of the girls indicated they spent time with them and since there were no charges pending, Hirsch didn't ask about the girls in particular. Just asked questions generally. Of course, they denied anyone getting drunk or doing drugs. The guys are underage anyway, so they were adamant there was no alcohol. None provided by them anyway."

"Right. And no way to prove them wrong." I took a deep breath. "Mitch, please tell me it wasn't Max's house they were renting."

He laughed. "That would be something, huh? No. Remember Dr. Montrose, that uptight woman? She moved before you left and has been renting it to students."

"No connection to the drugs or the murder."

"None. And even the girls' description of the party was pretty calm. No *Animal House* movie scene. Hirsch said the house was cleaner than he'd expected but not suspiciously sterilized. He said the guys were intimidated by the police showing up, though not sweating or avoiding questions. One of them wanted to know why all the questions, asked if someone got sick or something and started apologizing for the dip and using sour cream that was beyond the expiration date."

We both laughed. "Most of the students here have the money for drugs and there were some involved in drugs back when Justin Blake was killed. Any indications of that continuing or recurring?"

"Only rumors. One student hallucinating with evidence of drugs in his system a month ago. Another found unconscious with opioids in his system. Some tension among groups…" He shrugged. "…no clear indication it is drugs, but it comes up in cycles, usually around party times. If it's not one thing, it's another."

I shook my head. "Not good." An undercover officer might be needed at colleges, not just high schools.

"Anything else to share?"

"Not really. Things change and yet they're still the same. It's good to see you. I do have a staff meeting in a few minutes."

"Not a problem. It's good to see you and I hope you and Dora get to enjoy all your travels. You're looking great."

Mitch walked me out and gave me another hug with a cryptic "I'll be in touch."

CHAPTER 16

It was almost time to meet Kim, but I couldn't resist. With a lingering sense of nostalgia, I had to walk through the Arboretum. It was one of the things I really missed about Cold Creek. It was as calm and quiet as I remembered it. The fall flowers and turning leaves added to the beauty.

I'd leaned over to get a better look and smell a flower I didn't recognize, when I sensed someone coming up behind me quickly. The person plowed into me, knocking me off my feet. As I rolled away, I caught a glimpse of black boots and a purple motorized skateboard as the person took off. No one else was around and I tried to shake it off, only to catch my breath and not scream when I tried to put my weight on my left foot, and fell back down. My phone beeped. It was Kim.

"I'm out of class. Where are you?"

"In the Arboretum. Someone knocked me over and I think I sprained my ankle when I fell."

"Stay there. I'm on my way."

I twisted around so I would see if anyone approached and texted Brett, "Clumsy as always. May have a sprained ankle. Will update you."

Brushing leaves and debris off my jacket, I tried to keep my leg and foot still and checked myself for any other injuries. My left elbow was sore and likely would be bruised, but I had mobility. After a quick look in the mirror app of my phone, I worked on getting leaves out of hair, finger combing as best I could.

Kim jogged toward me. "Are you okay? You've only been here less than a day."

"Accidental I'm sure. The guy was on one of those motorized skateboard things, in a hurry, and the skateboard probably hit a twig or something and he control of it."

"Sheridan, anyone else knocked over? It could be an accident, but not you. And, if it was an accident, why didn't the person at least yell 'Sorry' as they glided away? Let's get you up and checked out."

We got me standing and then with Kim's help made it to a bench. I sat down and started to take the shoe off.

"You know, if you take the shoe off, you might not get it back on. Leave it. It's only a short hop to the entrance."

I nodded, thinking to myself how much longer than that it was to her car or my car. We slowly made it with me hopping and Kim lending support. I gave her a look as I spotted a student and a collapsible wheel chair at the entrance.

"You can't hop all the way to the car, now can you? Last year, it was decided every building should have a wheel chair. I thought it was pretty silly at the time. Now, it seems very convenient. This is my student and grad assistant, Alissa. Let's get you settled and we'll be on our way."

"Thanks, Alissa." I moaned as my foot touched the foot rest. Kim thanked her as well and took control of the wheel chair.

Getting to the car was not a problem, except when the chair bounced. Getting into the car was another story. Kim rambled on about Alissa and the class she'd just had until we were in the car and on our way.

"Okay, so where were you today and who could have followed you into the Arboretum. I'm not buying this was an accident."

"Honest, I didn't bug anyone. I sat with Max while they searched his office. Saw you and got coffees, talked to you and Brett in the hallway, went to Max's new house. Before you ask, they didn't find anything anywhere to implicate Max. Hirsch and I left there and we met up with Brett and Fabry at the Grill."

With a shrug, I continued, "We ate lunch and then they took off. I walked around the town center and then visited with Mitch at the counseling center. His student worker and two students saw me there. I had time before meeting up with you and went for a walk in the arboretum."

"Why did someone knock you over?"

"Kim, I told you. Accident and rude. They didn't apologize or ask if I was hurt. They also didn't threaten me in any way."

"Okay, okay. Here we are." She pulled into the drive-up entrance and helped me get out of the car and back into the wheelchair. "I'll meet you inside. Wait, you don't have your purse? ID?"

I smiled. "All under control. Wallet."

She nodded, hopped back in the car and took off and I entered the hospital. By the time she joined me in my cubicle, I was in the ever-stylish gown, my pants and boots removed with cold packs on my ankle and wrapped around my elbow.

Kim carefully folded my pants and I thought to myself "No way are skinny pants going to make it over that ankle." She looked at my leg and shook her head.

"You should've worn a skirt. I'll call Marty. I know just what he needs to bring."

An orderly came in. "Mrs. Hendley, we're going to x-ray now." With that, he wheeled me away and Kim added, "I'll find coffee."

And she did. Sort of. Marty and Kim waited for me back in the cubicle with coffee and a variety of clothes from Kim's house. We chatted and discussed the clothing options. A loose-fitting dress was the most likely solution, even if it would clash with my jacket.

The doctor came in, took in my visitors, and provided the findings. "Ms. Hendley, your right elbow is bruised, and you have a sprain with a possible hairline fracture of your left ankle. Here are your prescriptions, including one for a brace of sorts to keep your foot and ankle aligned, for crutches, and one for a knee walker scooter."

He paused and then continued, "I'd recommend the latter so you don't aggravate the elbow. Ibuprofen for pain. Ice, elevation and no weight on the left foot. You should follow up with your PCP in a few days if the swelling doesn't go down, in a week or two for updated x-rays." He turned around and left.

I looked at Kim and Marty. "Doc didn't know much medicine toward the end there, but he was more personable. Is Dr. Personality always like that?"

The nurse walked in and gasped as she caught the conversation. "Dr. Trask is not known for his bedside manner, if that's your question. Medically, he's good though."

She brought what I would best describe as a cast that you could strap on. Navy blue, soft and stiff at the same time. "I need to put this on. Your pants?"

"No. I'll be wearing a dress, I think. Can I take that off and on, like to take a shower?"

"Yes, but only with help. No weight bearing at this point as per the doctor's orders."

Marty stepped outside the curtain. The nurse made sure the curtain was closed and put the navy boot on and secured it. I clenched my teeth as she moved my foot.

"Thank you, I think."

She nodded and disappeared. Kim helped me change. By the time I had on her dress and one regular boot along with the blue one, the nurse returned with crutches, the knee walker scooter, and a wheelchair. She and Kim helped me stand so the dress would cascade down.

Wincing, I was situated in the hospital wheelchair and on my way to Kim's. Marty followed behind with the collapsible wheelchair, the crutches, and the scooter. He also called Brett to tell him the status and where we'd be.

CHAPTER 17

With my foot raised and wrapped in ice, plus ibuprofen, I lounged at Kim's while I waited for Brett. He had texted twice already, and although I wasn't in the mood for socializing, skipping dinner was not an option. I texted Melina and Maddie to let them know it would be after dinner before we got back to Clover Hill.

While the three of us waited on Brett's arrival, we caught the updates on the news. Not very informative and that made sense. Global statements about possible leads in the case, undisclosed persons being investigated, updates as possible. I shared what I knew and hoped Kim or Marty could add to it.

"Have you been to Max's house? It is huge and beautiful and fully landscaped. He – no, Stella – said it was a Moss Builders home. And that it was less than what they'd have paid for a house here in Cold Creek."

Kim shrugged. Marty tapped his chin and opened his mouth. "I've heard of them. They bought up land and subdivided it into different lots. A client asked about them and the restrictions." He paused. "What I remember is the usual language about mineral rights and ease ways. Then restrictions on how much of the land could be cleared. The bottom line was that although the buyer owns the land, the only trees that could be eliminated is what was needed for the house."

"I don't understand." It sounded very complicated to me.

"Effectively, the owner is restricted from adding on or even chopping down a tree – unless it is determined to be dead – to build anything else. Greens protection. Moss can build there, but not beyond limits set to preserve nature."

"How many houses have they built?"

"What Stella said was six. As we drove there though, we only spotted one. She said they were well hidden. I guess that's part of keeping much of the forest intact."

I shrugged, hit my elbow, and cringed. Kim got me another ibuprofen and I took a short nap. I awoke to voices, including Brett's and Fabry's, and momentarily forgot why I was napping as I tried to put weight on my foot. Not happening. I used the scooter to reach Brett.

"Woah! On that scooter you could be dangerous." Brett took me in his arms and shook his head. He was right though. If not for the pain in my foot, the scooter was much more fun than a wheelchair.

"Come on, you two. Marty put the steaks on and everything else is on the table. Sher, can I get you a glass of wine?"

I nodded and Brett arched his brows. "No pain meds, only ibuprofen. Besides, I'm not driving."

As we waited on the steaks, I repeated the story of the person on the skateboard. It didn't make any sense to me, but I had to agree, with my history, it probably wasn't an accident.

Over dinner, Brett and Fabry brought us up to date. Sebastian Cabot lawyered up and wasn't saying a word. Skinner was nowhere to be found. They'd gotten a search warrant for the Cabot house but that was not productive. He worked in securities and getting a search warrant for his office was taking longer.

"The only person we talked to was Mrs. Landry. Mrs. Celeste Landry. Now, she's a looker and Zoe was right, she dresses in designer clothes, not the kind of stuff you'd buy in a small town for sure." Fabry commented between bites and nodded to Brett. Not much got between Fabry and his food, though where he hid it was beyond me.

"She played the part of the grieving widow with the 'we were working things out' explanation of their relationship. Said she didn't like that Landry spent more time with his male friends than with her. She says she moved out to get his attention."

"Are you buying that?" Marty asked.

"Heck no. But her comment gave us an invite to talk about his male friends without giving up any information." Brett grinned and Fabry nodded.

"What did she have to say about the trio?"

"She didn't particularly like Jarvit. Described him as wild and into lots of things she didn't want to hear about. When asked, she said he was always talking about women, drinking, and cavorting with famous people."

"Wasn't that true for Landry, too?" I asked.

Fabry snorted. "I'd say so. Though she denied any knowledge of his involvement in drugs or anything illegal."

Marty shook his head. "What about Cabot? What did she say about him?"

"She didn't know him as well. She knew he was always part of the weekly breakfast and dinner meetings, but he didn't usually party with the other two or socialize. Mrs. Landry described him as laid back and easy to get along with. She did mention that the three men had been friends since college. They all attended Presidio College in Maryland. When I asked about who else he partied with, she clammed up."

"That's odd, don't you think?"

With a shrug, he replied, "Not so. From her expression, the person or persons who came to mind were of the female persuasion. If he was cheating on her, she didn't want to acknowledge it."

"No mention of drugs – other than alcohol?" Brett redirected the conversation.

Fabry paused in his eating to answer. "Nope. Like I said she denied that. But she did mention that sometimes he acted wired and must have started drinking before he got home."

"What about Jarvit?"

"Her description of him as wild could lead in that direction. The problem is, other than his association with Landry, we have no direct connection to the drugs."

"Presidio?"

Fabry grinned. "I looked it up. It's a very small private college that calls itself prestigious and clearly states not to be confused with the graduate school in California."

I shook my head. Brett cleared this throat.

"Speaking of college, did you manage to find out anything before you went to the arboretum?"

"I had a great visit with Mitch." Turning to Kim, I asked, "Did you know he's retiring the end of the year? Have you considered taking over the counseling services?"

Kim's jaw dropped and then she smiled. "No, I hadn't heard. Once he got that gig, he escaped the department craziness. I'll have to talk to him about that. He will be missed for sure. Did he know anything?"

I nodded. "Definitely some drugs at parties, for sure. He said there was only one instance with ecstasy that landed the student in the hospital that he knew about."

Fabry and Brett exchanged glances. "Two students ended up in the ER after taking a combination that included ecstasy in the past six months. The ER had Mitch's name on a handful of cases seen after parties. Mitch apparently brought one of the girls there and she was hysterical, in shock."

"He said the police investigated where the party was, but didn't get the impression – and had no evidence – that the boys who threw the party were involved or in the know."

"That's what we found out as well."

"Who else did you bother today, Sher?"

"I didn't bother anyone. Remember, I was with Max, and then Max and Stella. I walked around after lunch, visited with Mitch, and took a walk in the arboretum." I shrugged. It didn't make sense.

"You do have a reputation around here, you know? Someone could be spooked just by the fact you're here. Did you get a good look at the guy? Impression?"

"Black boots, purple motorized skate board, both feet on the board and he didn't stop when he hit me. My sense is that he was my height and maybe a little heavier, but not much. It was the momentum that knocked me over."

"Anyone see you leave the Grill?"

I shrugged. "No clue. But... Is there any indication of these designer drugs elsewhere? When I mentioned a possible drug connection – after it was on the news – one of the new profs at Millicent reacted and then found me later in the day to introduce himself. Asked questions and it seemed like he was fishing for information, but not doing a good job of it."

"Looking into all areas. Tomorrow, we'll be staying local in Clover Hill and checking with some of the students in the local high schools to see if anyone will tell us what we need to know. And checking with other townships and local police to see how widespread this is."

Kim nodded. "I can add a lecture on designer drugs to my next health lecture. Maybe that will prompt someone to come forward if they know anything."

"Education is important. Whether anyone will come forward as a result is another thing." Fabry shook his head.

"Hard to figure out. I still think the key here is Skinner. He's the weak link. Already been to prison. He won't want to go back." Marty added quietly.

We continued to chat as we finished eating. Brett tapped his watch.

"Hate to break this up, but we need to get on the road. We need to pick up Maddie and get Sheridan settled in at home."

"But I haven't had dessert yet!"

We all laughed. Marty added, "I'm afraid there's no dessert in this house. Kim keeps us both on a diet. I'll help get all Sheridan's stuff from our car and into your car, Brett."

Marty stood and cleared away dishes as he spoke and Kim did the same. Fabry pouted, but soon we were all outside.

"I wish someone had shown me the easy way to get in and out of the car without banging my foot in the process."

"Hold on." Brett slid the passenger seat back as far as it would go. "Now try. Slowly."

"It was great to see you and I'll get your dress back to you, promise." Hugs all around, I carefully climbed into the car. Thanks to the wine, I immediately fell asleep.

Brett woke me up when we got to Melina's to pick up Maddie. I opted to stay in the car and they all came out to see me.

"Sheridan, are you okay? What can I do to help? Can I sign your cast?" She gave me as much of a hug as she could with me sitting in the car.

I chuckled. "Maddie, I'll be okay, but, yes, I may need some help. I'm not sure if you can write on it or not. We can try when we get home."

Melina and Nedra took their turns at hugs. "Let us know if there's anything we can do to help as well. I'm happy to help transport Maddie wherever she needs to go."

"Thanks, Melina. I'll keep you posted."

CHAPTER 18

As awkward as the night time routine was, the morning was worse. First maneuvering in the shower, though Brett's assistance was much appreciated. Then getting dressed. None of my pants had wide enough legs to go over the brace and it was too late in the season for capris or at least that was my thought. As we looked at my dresses and the scooter, Maddie pulled out a pair of black capris and a jacket to match.

"Black is always dressier, Sheridan. And it's not supposed to be too cold. And this is a suit, right?"

I nodded and smiled. It was not the norm for her to be up early or to help me get dressed. And she was very helpful. She left for school and I pulled together what I needed.

"You sure you don't mind driving me? I could call in sick, you know."

He smiled. "Nope. This gives me an excuse to be in the area and casually stop and talk to the folks in Lynchburg. See if they're having an influx of these drugs over there. Put them on alert."

"Be sure to check at the Health Center and see if Craig Sims is working. My colleague Leah said he had some concerns."

He shook his head and continued. "Given what Mitch shared and the ER in Cold Creek, a stop at the ER also will be on my list. When do you get done?"

"No one wants to hang around on Friday afternoon. My classes are over at noon. I usually try to get grading done there, but I can leave any time after that."

"That'll work." He nodded. "I'll let you know when I'm on my way to pick you up."

It was a pleasant drive and we talked mostly about the changing colors. Hiking over the weekend was definitely out of the question. We pulled into the parking lot and Brett parked as close as he could. I got the scooter and he carried my backpack. I groaned when I spotted Dr. Addison as he waited for us at the doors.

"Good morning, Dr. Addison. This is my husband, Brett McMann."

"Pleasure to meet you. Dr. Hendley what happened? I'll have you know we are a fully accessible building. There is a handicapped restroom in the wing with my office if you need it."

His smile was forced and he kept glancing between Brett and me.

"Thank you, Dr. Addison. It's just a sprain. And whoever invented this scooter has my thanks. Much easier than a wheel chair."

The traffic in the parking lot was picking up and I looked to Brett for a way out of this conversation. "We better get you to your office, with a cup of coffee, before the halls get too busy. It was good to meet you, Dr. Addison."

"Good thought. Good thought. Let me get the door."

I was surprised when Dr. Addison didn't walk with us or offer to help me so Brett could leave. Maybe he was waiting for someone.

My office wasn't far and we made the stop to get coffee on the way. Leah's door was closed with a note about a faculty meeting. I pointed to the note. "That's why Dr. Addison was at the front door and didn't go to his office."

I opened the door and gasped. My office was in shambles. File drawers emptied, desk cleared off onto the floor. Brett immediately went into police mode and made me wait in the hall. I pulled out my phone and called the main office so someone could make the report to security. Dr. Addison would not be happy. In the meantime, Brett took pictures and pulled my chair out to the hall so I could sit down.

"Nice office. Very cozy."

I chuckled. "An oversized walk-in closet, but I don't really spend much time here. I think some of the offices are bigger. Leah's…" I pointed next door.

"…is maybe two feet wider. She can fit a chair at the end of her desk."

Security arrived. An older man, a bit portly, he lumbered to the door and looked in. His name badge read "Altuner" and he had a clipboard. He turned to Brett. "Dr. Handley, what can you tell me?"

"I'm not Dr. *Hendley*, she is."

He turned back to me and looked at the chair, the scooter, and then back to Brett. He cleared his throat. "No one indicated an injury when they called."

"It happened yesterday. You were called about the office. Someone made a mess." I got his attention and he turned back to me.

"I see." He slowly entered the office and made notes on his clipboard. "The inventory, other than the chair you're sitting in, matches what I can see. Is anything missing?"

"Not that I can tell. I'll have to check when I re-file everything. But yes, the furniture is all still there."

"Glad we can agree on that. When were you last here? When did you first notice this problem?"

Brett's face had gone from flushed to pale and flushed again.

"Brett, can you help me up and to the scooter, please? Then I think I'll be okay with Mr. Altuner here. I'll see if one of my students can help get the office back in order."

His mouth twitched and I leaned up for a kiss. Then he smiled. "Call me when you're ready to leave. Later."

He left with only one backward glance and a shake of his head, almost colliding with Leah. Leah joined Altuner and me.

"Who was that hunk? He's hero material. And what happened to you? And your office?"

I laughed. "That was my husband. If you're around when he comes back to get me, I'll introduce you. The sprained ankle, yesterday's news. The office? This is what greeted me today. And it looks like I have about 10 minutes to get my stuff together and go teach." I exhaled, no longer laughing.

"Hold on." Leah opened her office and returned. She started to pick up the stuff off the floor and looked at Altuner. "Don't just stand there, she needs to get to the desk. She at least needs a clear path." When he hesitated, she added, "Think OSHA violation."

He stood a little straighter, his eyes wide. I'd no clue an OSHA violation was that big of a deal, but it certainly motivated him to pick up stuff off the floor amidst grunts and groans. In no time, there was a path to my desk and I scooted in, backpack in tow. I opened it and pulled out my thumb drive and two papers.

"You need copies of those?"

I nodded. Leah took the papers from my hand. "What room are you in? How many students? I'll get someone in the office to make the copies and bring them to you. Lock the door, but I'd suggest you keep the backpack with you. Locks didn't stop that mess from happening."

"Thanks, Leah. I appreciate it." I gave her the information.

"No problem. I teach two classes back to back and then a break. I'll grab coffees and meet you back here to see what we can put this back together before we teach at 11 o'clock."

I nodded and she took off in one direction, and me in another. The class got silent as I scooted in. By the time I got the computer on and my lecture slides projected, a student worker came in with my copies.

CHAPTER 19

After class, one of the students offered to help me and I took her up on it. Lindsey was in both of my classes and a good student. She gasped when she saw my office and together we got the rest of the stuff off the floor and on the desk. I thanked her and began the process of putting things away, using the office chair to move stuff over to the file cabinet.

Dr. Addison showed up, not very happy. "How did this happen?" He looked at the lock on the door. He fiddled with the outside and the door unlocked.

"I think you just answered that question. On the plus side, I don't keep my grades or tests in here, if that's what the person was looking for. Just my lectures and handouts, articles on the topics, and granola bars. They did take the granola bars."

"You're not involved in that mystery are you? That's not what this is about? Why would someone steal granola bars?"

My jaw dropped and I had no response for him. Leah made her appearance with coffee and a dish of something yummy. "I got you a piece of the cake from the faculty lounge and a cup of coffee. Probably not as healthy as your granola bars, but…" She smiled and shrugged.

Dr. Addison cleared his throat. "Thank you, Leah, for being helpful here. Dr. Hendley, I'll have maintenance replace the lock by the end of the day. The key will be in your mailbox if you're not here to receive it." With that he turned and walked away.

"He must have been sucking on lemons. Did you get your copies okay?"

"Yes, and thanks for taking care of that and for the cake and coffee." I switched from the scooter to the chair, on top of the papers I'd set there, to enjoy my treats.

"Anything new on the investigation?"

"Not really. I'm sure you heard on the news about some leads and Dr. Addison's thoughts on the matter. They've pretty much decided this had to do with drugs." I shrugged. "Now they need to figure out who all the players are."

She stuck her head out my door before she spoke again. "Did Austin say anything to you after you met him Wednesday morning? He's been asking about you – a lot."

"That's odd. He stopped me in the hall before lunch. Introduced himself to me and checked me out with his eyes. Highly inappropriate. I mentioned my husband. Figured that might be a hint in case he was on the prowl. I mean really. I'm at least ten, maybe fifteen years older than him."

"And, obviously he thinks every woman will fall for his charms, but your husband? He's got Austin beat in the looks department and has more class besides."

"So, what was Austin asking?"

"Who you were… how long you'd worked here… where you live. Lots of personal questions. He also asked about the murder you were involved in and drug issues here and how you got involved. I was sorry I mentioned it. No one, including me, knew the answers to those questions. That was when you interviewed and no one has said anything since. Well, except Addison."

I chuckled. "And just what did Dr. Addison share?"

"Just what you said the other day. That you were told to not be involved in any more mysteries. As if he thought we'd all be running to you with mysteries to be solved. The biggest mystery here is usually how students could mess up in so many ways."

She hesitated and when I didn't say anything, she added, "But you are involved, aren't you? I can help. Do I need to spy on someone? Preferably not Austin, though. His office has a revolving door."

Having already dealt with one faculty member at Cold Creek College whose behavior violated every sexual harassment component and a few other laws as well, I cringed.

"If students had concerns, is there a counseling center or health center they could go to? I'm afraid I haven't really paid attention to stuff like that."

"You mean like to complain about someone? Like Austin? I don't think he messes with the students, only the faculty. If you rebuked him, he might be responsible for this mess. He's not used to being turned down if he shows interest."

"And you?" I watched for her reaction. Leah was on the short side with shoulder-length blonde hair. She dressed conservatively relative to younger faculty. Today she wore pants and a rust colored sweater.

"He has never indicated an interest and that's okay by me. Honestly, I'm fifty years old, with two grandkids and attitude. I'm one of the few women who actually questions what he's peddling on a regular basis. He steers clear of me most of the time. That's why I thought it was odd that he sought me out to ask about you."

"Definitely." I hesitated and then decided to go ahead and ask the question. "Anyway, that wasn't why I asked about services. When I was in Cold Creek, someone mentioned Roofies and how available they were. Frequently showing up at parties. Murder aside, I take issue with drugging someone without their knowledge."

"Wow. I haven't heard anything about parties or Roofies in particular. Kiera said something a few months back about clubbing and admitted she'd had too much to drink. She didn't remember getting home, but she had an Uber receipt. Her aunt, Claudia, lit into her about the need to be careful when she went out, you know, go in groups or at least with one other person, and so on."

"Scary to not remember and not know what you did. I hope she pays attention to her aunt's advice. Any idea where a student in that situation would go?"

She shrugged. "I guess they'd go to the Health Center – I mean that's how Craig would have seen any drug use. I'll find out. There may be some other places to go. It's never come up. Well, other than that one student earlier this year who flipped out. Hallucinating. That was a 9-1-1 call. They put him in an ambulance and took him away. Come to think of it, no one ever said what caused it or what happened to him. He wasn't in any of my classes."

As we talked, I had sorted more papers and pulled out the stuff I needed for my next class. I texted Brett to check on the student who left in an ambulance. And on one Austin Antos. My next text was to tell him I would be ready to leave a little after noon. He responded with a thumbs-up emoji.

CHAPTER 20

Brett found me in my office, with the mess almost cleaned up. Now it just looked like I had a messy desk. And other than the granola bars, I couldn't tell anything was missing. I'd packed up my backpack with what I needed for Monday's lectures. It didn't make any sense – what did the person think was in my office?

After I closed the door, he jiggled it much as Dr. Addison had, with the same result.

"Dr. Addison said they will replace the lock by the end of the day and leave me a key."

He shook his head. "And where is he leaving the key?"

"In my mailbox in the main office. Hopefully, in an envelope that's not too obvious. I imagine though he will write 'key' on the envelope. They won't find anything anyway."

He nodded. "Let's go. We have time and I fancy a quiet ride in the hills with my wife. I even picked up lunch and located a park nearby where we can eat." His eyes twinkled as he smiled.

"Playing hooky are you?"

"Not quite. Taking a longer than usual break. I don't have to meet Fabry for a couple of hours. And we need to talk about your texts."

"Did you find out about the young man they had taken to the hospital?"

"I did and I talked to him and his parents. A freshman. He and his parents decided he needed some time so he withdrew. He was sheltered and stressed at starting college. He was hanging out with some other students and one of them – he says he can't remember the guy's name – gave him a capsule with comic characters on it. Told him to chill out and not be so stressed and the capsule would help. He obviously had a bad reaction to what was in it – ecstasy and other stuff. The drug screen came back with traces of multiple drugs. This was a homemade combo."

"From your grimace, I gather nothing else happened after that. No leads."

"That sums it up. His parents had him withdraw. He's scared to death and won't even take aspirin now. And he won't leave the house except to run. I gave them the names of some counselors to help him. Sad situation."

"Anyone else show up at the ER?"

"None with confirmed drugs in their system. I did stop at a women's clinic the other side of Lynchburg. One of the ER nurses mentioned it. Hush, hush since all the issues with Planned Parenthood. Not sure how anyone at Millicent would know about it honestly. They weren't particularly open in sharing any information until I made it very clear all I wanted to know was if they had any indication of drugs involved in what brought the women to the center, not their identities."

He hesitated. "They finally acknowledged there were suspicions among the staff but no way to prove it. The women ranged in age and all came in suspecting something and not remembering much after a certain point, in a public place or party. That's as far as it went."

I shuddered. I could not imagine waking up somewhere and not remembering what I'd done or said or where I'd been for a block of time. Obviously, black outs are not uncommon in conjunction with alcoholism, but this seemed much more personal.

"Did you talk to Sims at the Health Center?"

"I did. He was very careful to not quite answer my questions. Apparently, it isn't just Dr. Addison watching out for the public image of the institution. He answered in generalities, with a little more. 'It is not uncommon for students to come in after a big weekend with a range of concerns, which could be construed as drug use.' He clarified he was not able to discuss them as related from a statistical perspective.

Coincidence, not causality." He shrugged as I grimaced.

"Now a question for you. What prompted the query about Austin Antos?"

I shook my head, still grimacing. "The first time I met him was earlier this week in the faculty lounge. When I made a comment about drugs involved with the murder, he blanched. Remember, I mentioned it before. Later, he made a point of stopping me in the hall with a comment on how we all had to stick together. He made my skin crawl. My take? He's a womanizer – a younger version of Adam and why he was killed. Today, Leah told me he was asking questions about me and my involvement with the murder and drug bust in the past."

"Reasonable explanation. Dr. Antos has never been arrested. No record. He was mentioned in a death notice. His wife overdosed. She had cancer. The coroner questioned if it was suicide. Antos didn't argue with that conclusion. He had been out of town at a conference and the cleaning lady found her."

"I guess that could explain his reaction to the mention of drugs."

"It could. On the other hand, his background was a little sketchy. In particular, what was listed on the college webpages didn't quite match with what the quick background check found. That is cause for doing more digging."

He nodded as we pulled into a park. I wasn't too sure how my scooter was going to work on uneven ground and hesitated getting out of the car.

Brett winked. "I checked it out in advance. You'll see."

He picked me up and carried me just inside the tree line where there were picnic tables. He sat me down and with a "Be right back" he was gone. He returned a few minutes later with a box filled with take-out bags, coffees, and waters.

"How nice. Thanks for thinking of this. It's beautiful out here." I leaned over and kissed him. Who says romance has to end after the wedding?

"And we have chicken salad, chips, and your choice of water or coffee."

I chuckled. "Both. Look at all the chicken salad on this sandwich." I took a bite and smiled. "Almonds in the chicken salad. Good."

We enjoyed our lunch without talking about the murder, though going back to Cold Creek on Sunday was a point of discussion. We still wanted to see the foliage and follow up with Kim. Brett packed everything back up and took it to the car or trash receptacles before carrying me back to the car. On the way home, Kim called.

"Hi, Sheridan. Marty is going to kill me. I've been sleuthing."

I chuckled. "What do you mean?"

"I looked up information on Moss Builders. There was an open house this afternoon in North Shore. I thought that was odd, but who am I to say. I went."

"And?" I put the phone on speaker so Brett could hear what she had to say.

"I think it was the same general area where Max lives. And it is beautiful up there. The house was huge and staged with very expensive furniture. Only a man and a woman were there. They were very cordial, though I got the impression they weren't really expecting anyone. Caught them in a kiss." She laughed.

"What did you tell them?"

"That was easy. I told them I owned a home in Cold Creek and my partner and I were thinking that maybe we needed a bigger house. Playing to their ego, I told them I'd heard good things about the houses they're building. Nice day for a ride and all." She paused and then continued.

"The woman gave me a tour while the man made a phone call. Odd, neither of them introduced themselves. I heard her call him Chase. Anyway, the house was gorgeous. In response to my questions, she said there were six houses already built – this was the sixth. The plan was to build two more. If I preferred a different floor plan, those hadn't been built yet. I mentioned the murder and wasn't the body found nearby. She paled and I was afraid she was going to pass out."

"What did she say?"

"Nothing of note. She excused herself and left me upstairs. I waited a few minutes and heard her telling Chase what I'd said. His voice was muffled and I couldn't hear what he said. I tried to be nonchalant and poured on the flattery about the house. Then I asked if they had a detail sheet to share with my partner. They gave me one, but get this – it was not for that address."

"Kim, did either of them give you a business card? Is there a name on the detail sheet?" Brett took over asking the questions.

"Only Moss Builders. Not an individual name."

"What did Chase look like?"

"He was okay looking, balding, average height. He was dressed casually, polo shirt and khaki pants. Leather jacket on the chair."

"How old do you think he was?"

"In his thirties, I think.

"Anything else you noticed about him? Anything that stood out?"

"For a realtor, he wasn't friendly or welcoming. The house looked beautiful, but the two of them weren't exactly in selling mode."

There was a crash, a screech, and Kim let loose a string of profanity.

"Are you all right? What happened?"

"Someone threw a brick through my window. There's glass everywhere. I'm going to call the police. I'll talk to you later."

CHAPTER 21

The call ended and I shook my head. "What do you make of that or of Chase? Do you think it's the same Chase?"

Brett's face was grim. "Maybe. Maybe not. I'll shoot her a picture of Chase to be sure. But then who was the woman?"

"Is it possible it was Celeste?"

"Celeste didn't have much positive to say about him. Of the two of her husband's friends, she liked him the least."

"I don't want to sound as cynical as Fabry, but couldn't she have lied?"

He chuckled. "Good point. One we'll have to follow up on. I'll talk to Fabry about it later." He pulled into the driveway and helped me out of the car and on the scooter. At the house, we were welcomed by the dogs and Brett let them out.

"Fabry is spending the day at the high school and Clover Hill Academy. He's going to have a talk with Caleb. See what he knows or doesn't know. He'll check in with the Stories boy who hasn't graduated as well. Then he's going to talk to a couple of random people at Clover Hill Academy and see if anything shakes out." Clover Hill Academy was the choice of many families who thought themselves above sending their kids to public school. Caleb and Luke had both been involved in the murder of Lawrence Stories and drugs in the past.

"Is there anyway there's a Buchanan in the mix? Mrs. Chantilly made a comment about the drugs and asked me that. She said Blake was upset about the murder and possible drug connection. Anyone talked to Shane recently?"

"I don't know about Shane. I was going to suggest you not go to Pets & Paws tomorrow, but maybe Mrs. Chantilly will be there and you can casually make a comment and see her reaction. Somehow that seems to work with you."

I nodded. Conversations with Mrs. Chantilly didn't always make sense. Sometimes she rambled and scrambled content. In the process, she might let something important slip out. It had happened in the past. I was never quite sure if that was intentional or not.

"We can do that, though I'm not too sure how much I can do. For now, I'm going to take a quick nap before Maddie gets home. And I want to check in on Kim before dinner."

"In the meantime, I'm going into the office to work on reports and such. We need more information on all the players. Landry to start with, then Cabot, Jarvit, and our good friend Jared Skinner. And maybe some information on who, if anyone, is in contact with Shane Buchanan."

After the nap, I felt better and popped into the office to find Brett on the phone. He finished the call and I pulled me, scooter and all, over to the desk.

"While I was up in Lynchburg checking things out, James took on the Buchanan clan and the high schools. We already knew Luke's story and needed to check on Caleb. Del Buchanan and his wife were a bit put off when James showed up at the house. Did you know Caleb's only attending half-days and is still at the Academy? I thought both of them were at Clover Hill High."

"Huh. I thought so, too. Why only half-days?"

"According to Del and his wife, he's on furlough at home Monday through Friday to attend school and returns to rehab for the weekend. A transition period was the recommendation from rehab so as not to over-stress him and allow him to gradually return. You're the psychologist here. Does that even make sense?"

"It does, sort of. Usually, they would have him home for the weekend first and then add days."

"They apparently did the weekends only and then switched to week days only when school started.

Now, he is five days home and two at rehab, but only for half days in school."

"Okay. For any student who is hospitalized, regardless of the reason, and therefore absent from school, friends, and so on, it is better for a gradual transition. With chronic illness, there is an issue of fatigue as well. I'm not sure how that works with drug rehab. It's conceivable that after not being engaged in school for several months, he could fatigue easily and not be used to constantly having to pay attention. In all likelihood, he's also behind academically and that would cause additional stress. And stress could be a trigger for drug use."

"That's kind of what they explained, in between accusing Fabry of looking for a scapegoat. Then Blake showed up. Fabry says he kept explaining they were talking to lots of students at both high schools. They called Caleb's attorney and his probation officer. Both listened in, along with Blake, Del and his wife, as Fabry asked his questions."

"What did Caleb say? Anything?"

"Nothing very productive. Fabry described Caleb as pale. He must have lost weight as his clothes were baggy and looked too big on him. He was serious and spoke slowly. Fabry didn't see anything to suggest Caleb is taking any drugs – medicinal or otherwise."

"That's good."

"Caleb stated the hours he attends school and which classes he is in, all of which is tracked anyway. He was hesitant to say anything else until his probation officer and lawyer prompted him to tell

Fabry if he knew anyone who might be involved. Told him it would look good for him if he cooperated. Odd thing? Blake didn't say a word at that."

"Will it help?"

"Not exactly. Not cooperating, however, would be a red flag and could hurt him. So they overstated the positive. Caleb wasn't comfortable though providing names with the audience he had. Smart boy. He asked everyone but Fabry to leave and asked the probation officer to end his call."

"I bet that went over well." My tone conveyed the sarcasm.

"As expected. Del and his wife caved first – if that was Caleb's wish, they'd leave. Probation officer complied with a reminder they would be talking on Monday. That left Blake. Fabry threatened to have him arrested for obstruction if he didn't leave. Not sure that would really hold up." Brett shook his head before he continued.

"Caleb's attorney – who is also Blake's attorney – told him to leave. Caleb provided two names he suspected were using or dealing. Just like with Luke, Caleb has been approached."

"And now, if Fabry talks to them, they will know, or at least think, Caleb had something to do with it."

Brett chuckled. "You don't know Fabry in the field. He showed up at Clover Hill Academy, flashed his badge and asked the principal to identify the students who would know the most about any rumblings in the school. So the first boy he spoke to was the Senior Class President, then the Junior Class President, both of whom were of age and didn't need a parent present." He paused for a sip of coffee.

"Then, he asked the principal for a list of other students and 'randomly' selected three names. The principal sat in on the three others, all underage, and Fabry kept his questions pretty vague. 'We're investigating designer drugs in high schools in the county. Have you heard any talk about ecstasy or Roofies or homemade combos in capsules with cartoon characters?' and the like."

He finished his eggs and shook his head. "The principal, of course, assumed the same questions were asked of the other two students. On the plus side, he assured Fabry there would be a special assembly on the problem and risks, and asked for suggested speakers. Fabry obliged."

"That's good." We both turned when we heard the door open. Maddie joined us.

"Dad, were you the one at the high school today, talking to students?"

"Not me, Maddie. Fabry. How'd you know about that?"

"Dad, really, with social media, there are no secrets. What's for dinner?"

"Pizza. We just need to settle on what we want on it." Pizza ordered, delivered and eaten, I called Kim.

"How are you doing? What did Hirsch say?"

"He shook his head and asked me who I made mad. Not much he can do. I wasn't looking out the window so I didn't see anyone or a car. Brett apparently talked to him and he showed me some pictures to see if I recognized the real estate guy. His picture was there. As I was leaving, a younger man arrived. Hirsch had his picture, too."

"What about your window?"

She snickered. "I cleaned up all the glass and then Marty had to vacuum the whole living room again, including all the furniture. He's at the hardware store getting wood to cover it and arrange for someone to replace the window. Good thing it's not too cold or raining. Here, he is now. Later."

CHAPTER 22

Maddie holed up in her room with the dogs and Brett agreed to watch a Hallmark mystery movie. It was a good one, but I realized our conversation on what Fabry found out had been interrupted. As soon as the movie ended I blurted out, "Okay, what about at the high school?"

"Fabry gave the principal the same spiel and immediately asked to speak with Tyler Stories. Tyler wasn't exactly helpful. He clammed up, denied any knowledge and told him to check the academy where all the rich kids go or ask the jocks. The principal didn't have much to say either, only that Tyler hasn't been the same since his father's murder."

"That's too bad. I hope someone has prompted Lila to get him some counseling."

"Fabry mentioned he was going to call her and suggested the principal to do likewise."

"So, the high school was a bust?"

"Not completely. He talked to the captain of the football team and a few others the principal identified as students who might know something. Oddly enough, the principal only identified boys. That didn't sit well with Fabry so he asked to talk to the head cheerleader and one of the girls on the student council."

He paused for a sip of coffee. "The cheerleader evaded his questions completely and was quite defensive. The student council president hemmed and hawed and finally admitted that there were rumors. Designer drugs are available at the high school – only she wasn't in the know on who had them and didn't want to know."

"That's not very helpful."

"No, but it tells us it's not limited to Cold Creek or Lynchburg. The principal was not happy with what he heard and Fabry gave the high school principal the same contact information for a speaker. Fabry asked him to identify some other kids most likely to be in trouble and made like he was selecting random names…"

I shook my head. "The principal mentioned Luke, right?"

Smiling, Brett nodded his head. "He did, but indicated he had expected Luke to be trouble, but so far no indication other than when he fell asleep in class after working all night at Pets & Paws."

That made me feel good and said a lot about Luke and the principal. "So what did Fabry find out from the supposed 'bad boys' the principal identified?"

"Not much. But he made sure they knew the police were on it and if they heard of anything or knew anything, they should contact him. And Fabry did one other thing – to protect Luke, he included him in one of the groups. Later, he stopped at Pets & Paws to check on him."

Brett chuckled and then continued. "He said Luke was okay and then asked about the vet. Is she married? He wants to know."

I laughed. When we first met, we'd joked about all the people in our lives who, once "coupled," decided everyone should be so happy. It was true. Whether it was Kim and Marty or Angie and Eric or most recently Fabry and Vanna, we seemed to project our romantic warm feelings onto them. Whether they liked it or not was another story.

"Where does that leave us?"

Brett's eyebrows raised. "Us? Haven't you and Kim learned anything yet?" His eyes twinkled and he squeezed my shoulder.

"Just consider me a sounding board. Let's start with Landry, the victim. Married to Celeste, friends with Cabot and Jarvit. Talks a lot about developing Cold Creek to bring it into the next century. What else?"

"You pretty well nailed it, Sher. He made his money in development. He took a concept and then sold it and franchised it to others. He's the one who brought all the new restaurants and a few boutiques to North Shore. And at least a few boutique stores in Cold Creek."

"I noticed the new stores. But how does that make money?"

"He puts together the start-up and then finds someone who wants to be their own boss, a small business owner. He shows them how this idea worked somewhere else, how much money other owners are bringing in, and they buy into it. Like any other franchise – from McDonald's to Starbucks – or in his case Eggspot and a few others. He's expanded and moved around in the last few years. Currently, he seems to be working the more rural areas."

"I bet it's easier to sell the idea in some place that doesn't already have five coffee shops. Okay, so he makes money by convincing others that if they work his idea, they can make money. Could one of those 'franchises' be drugs? What was in the box shipped to his house?"

He laughed. "An odd combination of over-the-counter pain relievers, tampons, opioids, roofies, and ecstasy. When the box was opened, it initially looked like a false positive – like the dog had been mistaken. Each box was opened and the contents checked. Someone had done a very good job of opening and resealing the packages."

"I'm not sure I understand."

"Some of the pain reliever bottles really held ibuprofen. Some didn't. When the package was opened, the pill bottle was no longer sealed and the contraband was inside. It wouldn't have shown in an x-ray. If the dog hadn't reacted to the box, just opening it? It would have looked like someone was stocking up."

"Knowing the contents for real, was it for his own use or to deal?"

"If that was the second box in two weeks, I'd guess to deal. One box over several months? I might go with individual use. Use might even explain the traces of various drugs in his tox screen."

"And you said he had a suspected history of drug involvement. What happened there?"

"It's puzzling. He was arrested and it looks like there must have been a procedural issue. There was no resolution. Bottom line, he was released and eventually the charges were dismissed."

"Hmm. That's odd. What about Celeste Landry?"

"They were married right after Landry graduated. She comes from a well-positioned family, not unlike the Buchanans. She's never held a job, though she has drawn pay from Landry's business dealings from time to time. No children."

"Have you met her?"

"Tally was the one who located her and did the notification. We all were there when the search warrant was served. Other than prescription medications, including Percocet, there were no illegal drugs found. She had the script for the Percocet from surgery on her elbow."

"Were they officially separated?"

"Not from what she told Tally or Fabry. No legal documents had been executed. She had been staying at a hotel in Richmond and had returned to the house on Wednesday to try to work things out."

"And he's her alibi. How convenient."

Brett chuckled. "I definitely think Fabry's cynicism is wearing off on you."

I punched his arm. "That leaves Skinner, Jarvit, and Cabot."

With a shake of his head, he responded, "Not sure about Cabot. From all that we can find out, he is an old friend of theirs and has dinner and breakfast once a week. He may even advise them on their finances, though there is no official record of that. No indication of money changing hands and he is the only one not living in a house built and subsidized by Moss Builders."

"Ah. What is their involvement in Moss?"

"Based on the paperwork filed, they are the owners, Jarvit as primary. The property was filtered through Landry to Moss and then the houses and lot were paid for. Nothing illegal there."

"And where does Austin Antos fit in, if at all?"

"I don't know. We're working on it. In the meantime…" He put his arms around me, lifted me up and carried me to bed. "You give me quite the scare some times." He let me know just how much he cared"

CHAPTER 23

Getting in and out of cars was much easier by Saturday and there was less pain. Brett reminded me I needed to make an appointment to get my ankle checked and wrote it on the white board in the kitchen. Maddie was excited to see the new pups and Brett was happy to drop us off. We'd all forgotten about the steps to get inside though. Brett carried me and Maddie carried the scooter. The front door opened and Mrs. Chantilly came out to greet us.

"Sheridan, Brett, this isn't the threshold. Is this a re-enactment?"

Maddie laughed and moved the scooter forward.

"No, Mrs. Chantilly, I sprained my ankle and can't put weight on that foot." Brett put me down gently and I leaned onto the scooter as I answered.

"Okay, well we're glad you came. Dogs are good therapy for pain, you know. Good for whatever ails you, ask Luke."

"Is Luke all right?"

"Oh, yes, he's wonderful. It's the dogs that are responsible. Detective, are you helping out today, too?"

"No, ma'am. I'm off to run some errands. I'll be back around noon." She nodded and he gave Maddie and me each a quick kiss and left. We went inside and Maddie immediately disappeared to the mama and pups room.

"You know, dear, as you get older you need to be more careful."

"For sure. Anything new here? How's Cocoa?"

"Cocoa is doing very well. We haven't found her forever home yet or a foster. Luke has put her photo on social medium, whatever that is. You understand it. Lacie understands it. Luke understands it. Me? Nope and no desire to understand it." Lacie had lived and worked at the shelter years before but after her involvement in a murder, she had disappeared.

"Luke in the back? I'll grab a coffee and help him out."

"That would be good. All this drug business has him nervous. He's come so far. Even Blake agrees and of course his parents. Not like Caleb."

"Is Caleb still having problems?"

"He's doing good. He's more like his Uncle Shane and some of his friends, not like Sebby."

"Who is Sebby? I don't think I've heard of anyone called that."

"It's not important. You have the hunk of your life. I have to get the cookies out. Now the peanut butter ones and chocolate chips are from Maddie and Nedra – for people, not dogs. Sebby was always the smart one, respectful, too. He'd know which cookies to eat."

She disappeared and I shook my head. In the back, I spotted Cocoa and Luke. I scooted over to Cocoa and talked to her, her tail thumping in response.

"What happened to you?"

"Wrong place, wrong time. Just a sprain and doing much better. Other than talking to the dogs, I'm not sure what good I can be."

"Talking is good. Maddie in with the pups?"

"Sure is. She wasn't going to miss them. How about you? You holding on?"

"Yes, ma'am. Better than I was the other night. Everyone at the high school is talking about the detective and how they talked to a bunch of us. Everyone's a little on edge." His color was good and he wasn't shaking. Like Mrs. Chantilly said, the dogs helped him a lot.

"Luke, maybe you can help me. Mrs. Chantilly just mentioned someone named Sebby. I've heard that name before and can't place it."

"Maybe she meant Uncle Sebby."

"Wait. Sebby Buchanan?" When we'd looked at the Buchanan family history, there had been lots of sons – eight sons who had eight sons at one point. Each generation continued to have sons, with only two girls. Most recently, Lila Buchanan had married Lawrence Stories, the person killed by Shane Buchanan. I didn't know of another male member of the Buchanan family who wasn't a Buchanan.

"No. He's not a Buchanan, not related. Not really. He and Uncle Shane go way back – high school, I think. I may not have it right, but I got the impression he lived with Shane in high school. I think they went to the same college, too. For sure, he comes to some of the family reunions with the Buchanans from other areas."

"Huh. That's interesting. Thanks. Someone must have mentioned him in that context. What's he like?"

Luke shrugged. "Okay. Friendly, enough, but kind of a stuffed shirt." He snorted. "Caleb and I couldn't figure out how someone like that was friends with Uncle Shane. Anyway, let's get you settled and talking to the dogs."

I couldn't do much in the way of cleaning or walking the dogs, but Luke found a chair somewhere and I got the dogs after their baths instead of having them hooked to the wall. Nedra and Melina arrived. Nedra said hello and quickly disappeared to join Maddie. Melina and Luke worked out a system and I played with the dogs.

"Sheridan, I want to give you a heads-up here. Any minute Maddie will come flying in here." Melina laughed. "We're all going to Thistledown Farms tomorrow to the corn maze. Supposed to be the best around, though we've never been before. Nedra suggested it, so that means she'll be inviting Maddie. I just got a text from Angie – they're all on board. So…"

Melina didn't get to finish as Maddie rushed in and almost collided with her and the dog she was working with.

"Can I go? It's supposed to be the best corn maze and we'll have so much fun. And I won't be any trouble to Miss Melina. I promise."

"I think it could be arranged. In truth, I've never been to a corn maze." Glancing at the blue boot on my foot, I groaned. "You'll have to tell me all about it when you get home."

Luke joined us and we all laughed at the two girls bouncing up and down in excitement. The girls went back to the puppies. Cocoa tried to follow and Luke brought her back to me.

"I wish we could take her. She's beautiful and so sweet."

"You can say that again." Brett startled me as he put his hands on my shoulders. "Agreed on both counts. She is a beautiful sweet girl."

Luke nodded. "She is. And she needs a forever home. Dr. Barksdale is looking, too. I wanted to tell you something."

As Brett's face hardened, Luke put up his hand like a stop sign. "Nothing bad. The corn maze? It's a lot of fun, but part of the fun is getting lost in it. Ms. Melina, you and your husband will need to keep close tabs on them."

There was a crash and Luke threw the leash he held and sprinted in that direction. Brett turned to go and Luke yelled, "All is okay."

"What was he talking about?"

Melina and I filled him in. "Was there a hidden message there? I mean the maze people know how to find people if they get lost, right?"

Brett nodded. "And there are lots of people, adults and kids, going through the maze all the time. On a Sunday, with nice weather? The place will be packed."

"Any suggestions on how to best keep track, then?" Melina asked.

"An app on everyone's phone will be able to tell you where they are if you get separated. The kids may decide to go off on their own, but tell them to stick together."

"He's right, Melina. We both have that app though I never think to use it. Maddie has it as well." I pulled out my phone and showed her. She quickly downloaded it with a "thanks."

"We ready?"

I nodded and Luke grabbed the scooter for me. With a few parting words to Cocoa, I joined Brett at the front of the house talking to Mrs. Chantilly. Just to see what happened, I asked, "Did you tell Brett about Uncle Sebby?"

"Such a nice young man. Now, he's an investment banker, prominent businessman. I'm so proud of him. Like Lacie. I remember when he was in high school. Oh, there were such problems back then. Blake and I would discuss the problems his kids had and their friends, of course. Blake and I... well, never mind."

"Luke mentioned Uncle Sebby comes to family reunions."

"Well, of course he does. In high school, Sebby needed a place to live and moved in with them. Blake had four sons then – Brandon, Delaney, Shane, and Sebby. Now, you take care of that ankle. We need you here. Cookies in the oven, I have to run." She quickly escaped.

Brett blinked and shook his head. "Explain."

"Later."

Maddie joined us with a big hug for her dad. "You're the best dad. And, you're the best, too, Sheridan. Thanks for letting me go to the corn maze tomorrow."

I chuckled and waited to see what was coming next. It wasn't a long wait.

"You know, we will be leaving early in the morning. Miss Melina, she suggested I spend the night there, if it's okay with you two." She bounced on her feet and I burst out laughing.

Brett shook his head. "You stay here. I'll be right back."

"You know, it's not right that you spend time over there and Nedra never comes to our house."

She nodded. "How about next weekend, we plan something with Nedra and she can stay at our house."

"Okay. See what ideas you can come up with."

Brett joined us in time to hear the discussion. He nodded. "That's a great idea. And Melina is on board with Maddie staying there tonight. We will join them at Al's at 6 p.m. tomorrow night for dinner."

I nodded. Maddie squealed and ran to tell Nedra. On the way home, Brett filled me in on his morning.

"I talked to Hirsch this morning. Kim identified the realtor as Chase Jarvit from a picture array."

"She told me she identified the man, but not who he was. She said one of the other men in the array arrived at the house as she was leaving."

"Jared Skinner. Fabry is checking all his haunts. He's determined to track him down. When he does, he'll find out who Jarvit's lady friend was." He smiled and took my hand. "Assuming nothing happens, we get to enjoy an adult dinner and evening."

CHAPTER 24

Early Sunday morning, both our phones rang at the same time. When I finally realized Brett answering only stopped half the ringing, I answered, "Hello?"

"Sorry to wake you up, Sher. How's the ankle doing?" It was Kim, who should have known I wasn't always most coherent before coffee.

"Better, but not great. Doctor's appointment on Tuesday."

"Glad to hear it. Umm… Marty suggested maybe you and Brett could visit today. He was kind of cryptic, but mentioned Max having a meltdown. I'm not good at calming him down at all. Marty is already stressed about the window and now Max. Any chance?"

"Brett's on the phone right now. I don't know of any reason why not. The plan was to go for a ride and enjoy the fall foliage – I'm not up for anything more strenuous than that. I'll give you a call after I wake up and check with him."

"Sounds good. We figured we could take you guys to the new brewpub in North Shore. Maybe stop to see Max and Stella at the same time."

We disconnected and I watched Brett's face. His expressions flashed from surprised to sad to angry and everything in between. With his free hand, he pulled his fingers through his curls – a habit of his when he was stressed or puzzled.

I couldn't tell for sure who he was talking to or about what. His side of the conversation was limited to "I got it." "I see." "What?" "Gotcha" and other equally uninformative comments. Charlie and Bella followed me into the kitchen, where I started making coffee and breakfast.

He was shaking his head when he joined me. "What a complicated mess. Let me do that. You sit down."

I didn't need any encouragement. The scooter meant I'd been trying to break the eggs twisted to my side. A definite invitation for an accident. He took over the eggs and got the toast going as well.

"Fabry?"

He nodded and before he could say anything more, I added, "I'm dying to hear what you two have found out, but Kim and Marty want us to go down there, have lunch with them, and try to calm down Max again. What do you think?"

He nodded before he answered. "That could work. They may have some answers to fill in some holes… And we could enjoy the foliage at the same time."

I called and arranged it with Kim. By then, Brett had breakfast on the table and we both had fresh cups of coffee. "Okay, so spill. What did you find out? What are those 'holes' you mentioned?"

He chuckled. "You do love a mystery, don't you?" He paused for effect before he continued.

"Let's get ready. Fabry filled me in on a few updates. Hold on to your curiosity until we're on the road."

I wasn't thrilled. With help needed in the shower and getting dressed, it took much longer than usual. Once we were both ready, it was a quick stop for coffees for the road and we were on our way. I immediately started with questions.

"So did Fabry find out anything about Jarvit? Or any more about Cabot or Landry?"

"We got the warrant to search Jarvit's home and office, and the plan was to talk to him. When Fabry showed up at the office, warrant in hand, handler and dog by his side, the office manager was blasé about the whole thing. She told Fabry that Mr. Jarvit had told her to expect someone to come by, probably with a search warrant, and she should comply. He was out of town at a realtor's meeting, or so she said."

"That's unusual, don't you think?"

"Definitely. And we know where he was yesterday. Fabry talked to her for a while, and the dog and handler went through the offices. They didn't find anything. The receptionist was a talker though.

Jarvit is into just about everything. Somehow, with Landry dead, the receptionist, Sally, seemed to think that Jarvit would expand his business. His business, like Landry's, is all about real estate acquisition and then getting the right businesses in place with supports to get those businesses off the ground."

"Did he ask her about Moss Builders?"

"He did. According to Sally, Landry was the silent partner on that endeavor. On the other hand, Jarvit was the silent partner on the Eggspot and boutiques. Fabry had already pulled the paperwork on Moss Builders and some of the others. Landry is incorporated as CCL Incorporated and that is what shows on the paperwork for Moss along with Jarvit. Moss Builders is then listed on all the CCL stuff. That would be expected."

"Wouldn't CCL Inc. then become Celeste's? And everything goes to her, not Jarvit?"

"That would be the assumption and with no will to be found, that would make Jarvit and Celeste partners now. How much that's worth depends on the success of both Moss and CCL."

"North Shore is pretty small. How much could they grow it?"

"Not just North Shore. Fabry spotted various plans – North Shore, Alta Vista, Cold Creek... many of the smaller towns from Roanoke to Richmond. He couldn't see the labels on all of them, but Sally took a call and mentioned Sleepy Hollow. That puts him up in our area as well."

"Isn't his office where you thought you saw Skinner?"

"It is and so far we haven't been able to locate him. Sally told Fabry she hasn't seen him since early last week. Fabry is working that end and he's not letting go. Oh, and Jarvit wasn't home and no probable cause to forcefully enter his home. Sally said she'd call Fabry when Jarvit came in or if she saw or heard from Skinner." Brett shook his head.

Brett's phone pinged and the dashboard screen showed a text from Fabry. "Sally came through. On my way back to Jarvit's office to talk with the elusive Mr. Skinner. Later."

Brett responded with a thumbs up emoji. I laughed.

"Fabry smitten or only Sally?" Fabry was a nice looking man, even with a crooked nose. Although usually in gruff and grouchy mood, he could turn on the charm when he wanted.

"Only Sally. Fabry joked that his flirting netted more information than the drug dog and his handler."

CHAPTER 25

By the time our drive took us through wooded hills, the foliage grabbed our attention. One of the best parts of fall, the escape from the summer heat notwithstanding, the reds, oranges, and yellows created a continuous wave of color. We pulled in at Kim's house and Kim and Marty were waiting for us.

The large plank of wood on the front window made it hard to ignore what happened.

"It's so good to see you again. I know, I know, it's only been a few days, but it's like old times."

Marty shook his head. He looked nervous and I had to wonder what was going on with Max. Outside, he waved his arms at the wood covering the window and shook his head. Inside, he explained.

"Someone is throwing bricks at Kim and Max is hysterical. Now Max hysterical is nothing new, of course. Only I can't get him to keep his mouth shut. Any chance you solved the murder or officially cleared him so he will calm down? Or have any idea who did this?"

Brett opened and closed his mouth. "No, it's not solved. It looks like Landry's death is connected to something much bigger. That's the angle we're pursuing right now. That's all Max can know. He could shut down the investigation or make it difficult for us later on if he starts spouting half facts or his own thoughts on Landry. All we can tell him is that he should calm down and let the investigation continue. The more he talks, the worse he makes it."

"Sheridan, can you try talking to him? I'm very concerned about him."

"Okay, okay. I will try." I scootered away and pulled out my phone.

"Hi, Max. It's Sheridan. How are you?"

"Oh my gosh! Sheridan, I'm going crazy. Is your husband still trying to pin this murder on me? I don't know what to do? When are you coming back to Cold Creek?" He spoke quickly, almost yelling.

I chuckled. "We're in town today in fact. Drove down to enjoy the foliage and have lunch with Kim and Marty in North Shore."

"Your husband, too? I'm afraid he'll arrest me. Can you stop by without him?"

I chuckled. "Max, they checked your house, your office, talked to you and Stella. Nobody's still bothering you, are they?"

"Only Joe. He makes me crazy with his questions and innuendo and talk of drugs."

"But nobody official? Sounds like they've moved on. You need to let it go and keep quiet while the police figure it all out."

"Okay, okay."

"Will you and Stella be home later? Maybe we could stop by, just to visit."

"With Brett and he won't arrest me?"

"With Brett and unless you broke the law, he won't arrest you. A social call."

"I'll check with Stella to be sure, but that sounds good. We mostly stay home these days. I'm afraid when we go into town everyone is looking at us and thinking we're involved in the murder or someone said something about drugs."

"Just chill, Max. Let me know what Stella says and I'll see about what time would make sense."

He disconnected and I took a few relaxing, cleansing breaths. Talking to him was exhausting. I joined the others.

"…lot of talk about designer drugs on campus. Mitch made a lot of noise and got the Chancellor all riled up. We've been inundated with emails. Every class now has to have a speaker come in on the dangers of drugs and particularly designer drugs. Not all the students will be receptive and some will tune it out. Others will get the message." Kim shrugged.

"That's a good start." I moved to the couch and drank my coffee. I smiled as I realized they were all waiting on me.

"Max is… Max. We are invited to come by for a visit – as long as Brett doesn't arrest him." We all chuckled, except for Brett. He shook his head.

"He mentioned drugs, mostly in relation to Joe and his insinuations. I guess if the whole campus is talking about drugs now, that makes sense."

"That was definitely the topic of the day on Friday. Very little mention of the murder or even the search of Max's office on Thursday. And, honestly, I never heard anything to suggest Max was involved in the drugs."

Brett nodded. "Good. You and Sheridan can repeat that part to him – the big focus is on drugs now and not connected to him."

He didn't add, but I knew there was a "so far, at least not directly." He did ask, "Has Hirsch said anything about the brick incident."

Kim shrugged. Not much usually got her down. "Only the obvious. Even today's technology can't get fingerprints off brick. In the glass, I found a note when I swept it all up. In block letters, it read 'Mind your own business' and we assume it came with the brick. Hirsch has it."

Thinking about Landry and Jarvit, and the comments Zoe had made at the Grill, I asked, "Have you heard rumblings of new stores and restaurants in Cold Creek? Zoe made some comment about it at lunch the other day."

Marty cleared his throat. "Yes, a lot of rumblings at the courthouse. I don't mess with real estate or permits or zoning, but, yeah, a lot of talk – pro and con – about revitalizing main street with more options for everything. Potentially, even a mall."

"Can you imagine that? I am one shopper gal, but in Cold Creek? And I heard it would be mostly boutique-style stores, not major department stores. Something about the need to cater to the college population."

"You have to admit, Kim, many of the students are from the country club set and could afford high end clothes and accessories. Huh. That was the group involved with drugs the last time. Any of them likely to be involved this time?"

Brett leaned in as Kim hesitated to answer. "Not for sure. Not that anyone's sharing. A couple of them are obnoxious and self-centered, don't think they have to study, but nothing obviously drug-related."

Brett's phone pinged and he handed it to Kim. "This the lady at the house yesterday?"

"Oh my gosh. Yes, it is. Who is it?"

"Celeste Landry."

"That would explain why she reacted so badly to my comment about the murder. What was she doing there?"

Brett texted and then read the next text. We waited, not so patiently.

"Fabry is talking to Skinner and waiting on Tally. Right now just making conversation and asking about business. Like Moss Builders and the houses. Skinner named Celeste as the person who usually did the sales end. That's all I know and you just confirmed her as at the open house. Did you give them your name or address?"

"I signed in with my name and Cold Creek as my address. Not the actual address. When I left though, Jarvit made it a point to walk me out to my car."

Brett nodded. "He could have gotten your license and then managed to get your address that way or via the internet with even your name and Cold Creek. Definitely could have done it."

Marty cleared his throat and stood. "We have a reservation. I was able to add the two of you, but they are usually swamped for Sunday lunch. Let's go have lunch and then deal with Max."

CHAPTER 26

Continuing our notion of enjoying the foliage, we took the scenic route through the park and up the main highway.

"Have you eaten at this place before?"

Kim shook her head. "No. We had reservations last Monday, but had to cancel due to the road closure. Marty decided tonight would be good. It will be an adventure for all of us."

The foliage along the way was beautiful. In no time, we were turning off the main road and stopped for a few minutes to get some pictures of the forest from a ridge. I stayed in the car, but the view was breathtaking.

A little further down the road we entered the main part of North Shore. It had changed a lot since I'd been here last and I spotted the various new stores and restaurants. All somehow planned by Jarvit or Landry or both. Financed somehow as well.

Marty pulled into the parking lot of Leavitt's Brewpub. A rustic feel, simple and unpretentious, yet housed in an upscale building. A step above what I expected for sure. Marty still seemed very nervous and I worried about him. Max could get on people's nerves but this seemed over the top. The window and Max would be understandable.

Kim and I were talking when Marty gave the hostess his name and her face lit up. "Yes, Mr. Cohn, we have everything ready for you. Sorry you weren't able to make it last week."

She grabbed some menus and we followed her to the back of the restaurant. I noticed some of the waitstaff following us, but dismissed it. The table for four offered a view of the countryside.

"The view. So beautiful."

Marty pulled out a chair and Kim sat down, still enjoying the view.

"Yes, you are – so beautiful."

As he dropped to one knee, it became obvious why he was so nervous, and why there was a bucket and bottle of champagne. Kim screamed, he proposed, and when they sealed it with a kiss, we joined everyone else in the place in the applause. Amidst many well-wishers, we managed to eat a delicious lunch and put a dent in the champagne.

"Did you know about this, Kim?"

"Nope. He suggested a late lunch here because Monday was cancelled. Just lunch." She looked at him and smiled.

He chuckled. "It's been a long time coming and the next step in our relationship. I … I was a little afraid she'd say no."

Kim leaned over and kissed him. "I thought you'd never ask."

They both glowed and Brett took my hand and kissed it. "When is the big day?"

I burst out laughing when both of their faces went from smiles to wide eyes and a look of panic. "You have time to figure that out, lots of things to consider."

They both relaxed and we finished eating. Marty was going to leave the half-bottle of champagne and Kim vetoed that. With the champagne wrapped in a towel and secured in the trunk, a visit with Max was the next stop.

As we pulled into his driveway, Kim smiled. "Don't forget the champagne!" and I nodded at her choice of distraction.

Max barreled to the car as Kim grabbed the bottle and thrust it at him. "I hope you have glasses, Max. We're celebrating."

"What? Huh?" He looked at all of us smiling and ignored Kim's offering.

"Champagne, celebrating, ring?" Marty put his arm around Kim as she spoke. Brett did likewise with me. "Are you going to invite us in and share in the champagne or what?"

"Oh my gosh. Congratulations. Come in, come in." He turned and half-ran to the open door. "Stella, Stella, they're here. Come quick."

By the time we were inside, Kim still holding the champagne in a towel, Stella joined us. One look at the bottle and Kim and Marty, and she immediately caught on.

"Congratulations! You look so happy, both of you." She smiled at Brett and me and added, "You, too. Good to see you again under more pleasant circumstances. Let me get some glasses and dessert. Max, take them to the living room."

She disappeared and I asked Max about Joe once we were in the living room.

"He is … he keeps bothering me and wanting to interview me. I told him no like you and Marty said. Then he makes comments about drugs – this was even before the other detective and Chief Hirsch asked about them. He's like a dog with a bone, and no matter how many times I tell him I didn't use drugs in my lab, he won't quit."

"Did he mention any kinds of drugs? Any names?"

"He mentioned some . Some of the ones in the presentation the Chancellor says we have to show. I recognized some of those. Ruffles? Fantasy? I don't know. Drugs are not my thing. And he won't leave me alone. Not even after the police and detective went away."

"I'm sorry he's bothering you. Did he mention why he thought you might know about these?"

"The murder, of course. Don't you know? He said the murder was tied into a drug ring and that awful person who was selling drugs before and the murder you got involved in. You always were a magnet for murder."

Kim interjected, "Did he mention any names Max? That might help find the real killer."

Stella joined us with apple cobbler and champagne flutes. Kim poured, with most of the champagne going to Max and Stella.

He shook his head and started pacing after downing his champagne. "Oh, no. I wasn't paying attention to him, just trying to make him go away. Odd though, he asked about re-enactments of Civil War battles. I'm a scientist, not a historian. And the other murder involved with drugs. And security."

I nodded. Justin Blake was killed because he uncovered a drug ring among the country club set. His downfall was telling one of the security guards, who was involved in the drug trafficking. Marty leaned forward at the mention of the Civil War battles.

"Civil War re-enactments?"

Max shook his head and flailed his arms. "Were these drugs used in the Civil War? I don't get it."

"Okay, Max. Other than Joe, anyone else bothering you or Stella?"

He shook his head and Stella cringed. "No. I had to clean up my office and some of the students asked what was going on."

Marty refilled Max's glass and leaned back. "Max, from what you're saying, it looks like the investigation is no longer focusing on you. That should make you feel better."

"I don't know, Marty. You never can tell. No offense, Brett, but police want to solve cases and don't much care if the person is innocent or not. Joe reminded me of that on Friday. Told me I could still be in trouble."

My hand squeezing Brett's arm, I shook my head. "Max, he's just trying to get you riled up so you'll talk to him. How does he think you're connected to drugs?"

"I… I don't know. That's a good question. Maybe I should start asking him questions if he keeps bothering me."

"Well, I have a question." It was the first time Stella spoke and we all looked at her. "When is the wedding?"

That set us all to laughing. After a bit, I asked her to show me to the bathroom. "Lovely house, but I think I mentioned that when I was here Friday." I paused and added, "Stella, when I asked if anyone was bothering Max or you, you didn't answer. Is anyone bothering you?"

She glanced behind us before she answered. "Not bothering. Not really. Celeste Landry? Connor Landry's wife? She and some man came by asking if we'd received another package intended for Connor. I didn't know what to tell them. I … I told them the truth – we didn't have any packages for them, the police took the package."

I nodded. "Did they say anything else?"

"The man. He asked if I knew what was in the package. I told him I had no idea. The delivery guy showed up while the police were here and they took it. Mrs. Landry? She thanked me and wished me well."

"That was nice of her. And you did the right thing. What did the man look like?"

"Middle-aged, nicely dressed, balding – then again most men his age are balding. On the shorter side, like Max, not Brett."

I nodded. "Okay. You better go back and I'll be right there."

We left their home shortly after that. With lots of hugs and congratulations to Kim and Marty, Brett and I drove back to Clover Hill. I shared what Stella told me as he drove. Another time when Celeste and Jarvit were together.

My phone ringing with my mother's ring tone reminded me it really was Sunday and I had forgotten to call.

"Hello, mom. Did you and Dad decide about the cruise?"

"Oh, Sheridan, it's so exciting. We barely ever leave here and now we're going on a cruise. Kaylie is coming in this weekend to help me shop for a few things. Your father is still a little leery. I say too bad. We may never have this chance again. Play bingo. Entertainment. All the food. Dancing."

I chuckled. The last activity is probably what made my dad leery. "That's great. Anything else going on?"

"Oh, I don't want to jinx it. Kaylie is seeing someone new. Maybe…"

"That's good. You need to just let her move at her own pace." Meddling in our love lives had been one of my mother's favorite past times and we never seemed to get to the alter fast enough. I remembered being so careful not to mention Brett for a very long time. Safer that way.

"Is everything okay with you? Your job?"

"Yes, mom. All is good. Brett and I spent the day in Cold Creek and we're on our way to meet friends for dinner."

"Okay then, I'll let you go. I have to work on your dad's clothes and see if he needs some shopping. The cruise is only three months away."

"You do that and give dad my love."

Brett and I both laughed. She'd probably be packed two months ahead of time.

CHAPTER 27

We arrived at Al's only a few minutes late for dinner. Melina and her crew, Angie and her children, Eric, and Maddie were all talking, several different conversations going on at once. Not by accident, the six adults were seated at one end and the five children at the other.

"How was the corn maze? Did you have a good time?"

Maddie was quick to respond. "Great. Fabulous. Awesome. There was this huge cornfield and they'd cut paths in it. I don't know how they managed to do it. There was a picture of what it looked like from the air, but how did they know where they were cutting? The corn was so high."

Eric laughed. "At least one place I used to visit as a kid? They cut the paths when the corn was only a foot high. They had the maze all planned out to turn people around and put it on top of a photo of the cornfield. Then marked all the main paths first." He shook his head. "They probably use GPS now."

Willie nodded. "Probably. Creating blueprints or something like that. Same as they do with urban planning and mapping out roads."

"It was fun, especially when we got lost." Karla chuckled and pointed to her mom. "She was scared, but I wasn't. I knew someone would find us."

Angie shook her head. "There were lots of people. They try to limit how many can be in the maze at the same time and stagger when groups enter. The path is fairly even and the walker worked great. Not all the people coming behind us were particularly nice."

Karla's smile disappeared. "And they wouldn't let me take one of the dogs with me. Duke is getting old and he's the best." Duke was an unofficial support dog for Karla. If he'd been "official" they would have had to let him go with her.

"Karla did great though and we all found our way out. Even if some of us had to reverse, a lot."

They all nodded and started talking again. Eric shook his head. "I wish I'd been able to get out of my commitment to go with you."

Angie smiled. "We were fine. I wasn't worried as much as annoyed that some kids would push us out of their way."

"What's up with Duke? Is he okay?"

"He's okay, but getting older. And he is the one who really allows her to be outside. The other two aren't big enough."

"Would you consider getting another dog, a bigger dog."

Maddie must have been eavesdropping on our conversation and shouted, "Cocoa! She's great."

Angie shook her head. "I don't know. We 'inherited' the ones we have. I'm not sure it would work."

"I understand. Think about it. Maybe visit Pets & Paws and see what you think."

Angie looked uncomfortable and I intentionally shifted the conversation. "Willie, how's senior year?"

"It's good. I'm applying for scholarships and such. I want to study engineering, not sure where." He glanced at the others and his mom and then back to Brett. "Mr. Brett, can I talk to you for a few minutes?"

Melina almost popped out of her chair, only her husband, Vince, stopped her. He whispered, "Let him be."

Brett smiled. "Sure thing, let's check out the cars in the parking lot."

The others noticed them leave and Maddie asked, "Where are they going?"

"To check out the cars in the parking lot."

Maddie looked at Nedra and smiled. "Is Willie getting a car? Can he drive us places?"

Melina and Vince put the lid on that idea. Unfortunately, it brought up the inevitable "When can I learn to drive? Start to drive? Get a car?" directed at all the remaining adults from the three 15-year-olds at the table. All of us gave vague answers

165

and they all decided to talk about something else and ignore us.

"Sheridan, do you know anything about the situation in Cold Creek? I haven't talked to Marty in a while. Meant to call him, but, well…"

I smiled. "Eric, yes, Brett and I have been down to visit this past week and that's where we were today. When you get around to calling him, congratulate him. He proposed to Kim at lunch today."

"It's about time. I'll definitely give him a call later."

Brett and Willie rejoined us with some kind of fist bumping thing and the conversation died. Tired, I signaled our waiter for the check. It was time for the party to end. To test out my ability to drive, I drove us home and we decided I could drive myself to work in the morning.

Once Maddie was asleep, Brett shared his conversation with Willie. Willie knew about Fabry's visit and agreed that was all anyone was talking about. He told Brett he'd heard rumors and caught parts of conversations in the bathroom. Brett now had a few more possible leads on students who might be involved. Before going to sleep, he got a call from Fabry. As usual, I only heard bits and pieces.

I arched my eyebrows and stared at him as he disconnected. In return, he leaned over and gave me a kiss.

"Skinner connected Celeste and Jarvit, implied more than business. He heard an argument between Jarvit and Landry the week before the murder. He couldn't make out the words, but definite voices raised and then something breaking and then Landry storming out."

"Could he be fabricating it?"

"Sally confirmed and Fabry…" Brett chuckled. "…let her know how disappointed he was that she hadn't shared that."

I shook my head. "What else did Fabry find out from Skinner?"

"Skinner, by his description, was the errand boy. Go here and pick this up. Deliver this to this person. He was the 'set-up' guy for the open houses. As far as he knew the one Kim went to was cancelled, so he hadn't gone and turned on lights or the aromatic thing to make the house look and smell more inviting."

"Who cancelled it and why?"

"Now, the 'why' makes sense. Landry's death. Sally said she wasn't told to make any changes to the website, but she recalled a mention of no open houses. Therein was the miscommunication."

"Hmm. That means Jarvit and Celeste may have been trying to sort out the silent partner and joint ownership stuff and used that house as a private place."

"That's one explanation. Fabry made appointments with both of them for tomorrow morning. At Tally's office."

I nodded. "Skinner know anything else? Do you have a picture of him?"

"Hmm… yeah, here."

He handed me his phone. Skinner looked older than I remembered him. What struck me wasn't his overall appearance.

"See that purple thing in the background? Is that a skateboard? And he's wearing black boots. Skinner knocked me over."

Taking his phone, Brett enlarged the image and nodded. "He is wearing black boots and that is a purple skateboard with a motor. Guess we have another question for Mr. Skinner. He denied any knowledge of drugs. He's on parole and gets drug tested same as Caleb. He couldn't really admit to any knowledge. After his comment to Sally about being disappointed, Fabry asked her if she knew or believed that Jarvit might be high some days."

"What did she say?"

"She hesitated. Then she conceded there were times when he was 'off' or seemed more wired and angrier than others. It could just be his personality and other stuff or it could be drugs or both. Guess we'll find out more tomorrow. I'll be leaving early. Are you sure you'll be okay to drive tomorrow?"

"Yup. I don't use my left foot when I drive so the hard part is still getting in and out of the car."

He took me in his arms and eventually we went to sleep.

CHAPTER 28

A little worried about the drive, I gave myself plenty of time getting ready and on the road. For a change, I was arriving early instead of 'just in time.' The best news was that I didn't run into Dr. Addison. The bad news was the scooter made it impossible for me to open the front door and scoot in. One of the custodians spotted me and let me in. Thankfully, the main office was unlocked and the main admin, Ms. Sinclair, was there. An older woman, I'd had minimal interaction with her in the past year.

"Morning, Ms. Sinclair. How are you?"

"Morning yourself. You here to get the key to your office?"

"Yes, as a matter of fact, I am." I glanced at my mailbox and it was empty. "Dr. Addison said he would leave it in my mailbox..."

"And I told him that was silly. If he left it in your mailbox whoever broke in could just take the key and finish whatever they were doing." She walked around her desk and handed me a key.

"Here you go. It's been locked in my drawer and no one knew that. You be careful now. The young people today, they just don't have any respect."

"Thank you, Ms. Sinclair. I guess I better get going." I didn't think my office being trashed was the work of students, yet it was certainly a possibility. One that was easier to swallow than that it was another faculty member.

The halls were quiet with only a few stray students. I easily scooted to my office and the key worked. Then I faced the inevitable realization that I hadn't finished putting everything away on Friday. I set aside what I needed for my two first classes and then attacked the pile that still needed to be sorted and refiled. With about thirty minutes before class, I looked up as my door opened, expecting it to be Leah. It was Austin Antos.

"Who are you, really? What are you doing here?"

"Good morning to you, too, Dr. Antos. You already know my name. I'm a temporary replacement for Shelley deMiranda, a faculty member in psychology. She's on extended family medical leave. But I think you already know that."

"How were you involved in a murder then? You undercover or what? Do you even know anything about psychology?"

"I'm a licensed psychologist, Dr. Antos. I was 'involved' in the murder Leah mentioned due to family interests. I'm not sure why that should matter to you."

"I think you're the reason I'm being asked questions. You stay out of my business, you hear?"

"Dr. Antos, I don't understand…."

He turned and slammed my door as he stomped off. I slumped over, drained from not losing my cool or blurting out anything. Obviously, this was not his win people over look. Just as obviously, the questionable background check was an issue for him. Contemplating what that could mean, I jumped when Leah walked in.

"Sheridan, are you okay? I didn't mean to startle you."

I shook myself. "No problem. Lost in thought. How was your weekend?"

"It was good. Uneventful, but good. And yours?"

"Same, and the ankle is doing better. We'll see what the doctor says tomorrow."

"Need any copies made? I'm on my way to the office."

"Thanks. I have everything here for today, thankfully. The rest of the week? That's another story."

She laughed as she walked away. I gathered up my stuff and went to class early, avoiding the rush in the hallway.

The next time Leah stopped in was after her classes. I'd cleaned up and sorted and filed everything and I felt good about my office and job, temporary as it might be. From her grimace as she looked around and closed my door, Leah did not share that feeling.

"Leah, what's wrong? Sit down."

"Austin Antos. He just stopped me in the hall. He doesn't even teach on that hall. Asked me if I knew what you were up to and told me it was not in my best health to talk to you. That you were trying to ruin him and making up lies about him. I heard something like that from Kiera between classes as well." She whispered and kept looking back at the door.

I shrugged. "Odd. He came in here this morning – that's what had me spaced out earlier. Something about being asked a lot of questions and blaming me. He's giving me way too much credit for anything that's happening to him."

"Something is definitely going on with him, and he's angry. What do you make of it?"

"The only real reason most people would be angry about being asked questions would be if they were hiding something. Any idea what he could be hiding?"

She leaned back and shook her head. "No clue. They supposedly do background checks, but I don't know that they really look at them. To hear him talk, he was a successful business man, found it too stressful, and jumped at the chance to teach in a small college when he saw the position post. A transition in his career he called it."

"I assume he had the same or more of the interview process I had? How many applicants were there?"

"Well… As a small private college, we don't get a lot of applicants. He had to give a lecture and meet with everyone associated with the business program, I think. It was over the summer so not many people were around."

"And the position needed to be filled quickly… Is it possible they skipped the background check? And now someone is questioning it?"

Her eyes popped open and her mouth dropped. "Oh! That would be awful! I wonder if a student complained."

"Or another faculty member in business? I only met the man for the first time a week ago, and business isn't my area. I certainly wouldn't have an opinion on his qualifications. Personality? Oh, yeah. Especially after today."

She nodded. I glanced at the clock. "Last class and then home." I gathered up my stuff and opened the door slowly. I nodded the all clear and Leah left. An hour later, I returned to my office and opening the door found a note.

"Rumors in the lounge…Austin not who he claims. Call me. Leah" and her phone number. I put the note in my backpack and scooted myself to my car, half expecting to find it damaged. Cars and my being involved in a murder didn't seem to be a good match. This time I was pleasantly surprised. Doors were still all locked and closed and the tires still had air in them. And, it started right up.

CHAPTER 29

As soon as the dishes were cleared from dinner, Maddie ducked back into her room. I shared the note with Brett and called Leah.

"Hi, Leah, Sheridan here. Is this a good time?"

"Hi, Sheridan. Just playing with my dog, Trouble. You won't believe what I found out."

I chuckled at the dog's name. "Tell me."

"It's all anyone could talk about. Austin mispresented himself on his vita. It was all a bunch of lies."

"Like what?"

"First off, he doesn't have a doctorate. He had that he'd graduated from a prestigious business school in California. Only he didn't. He got his undergraduate degree from some small liberal arts school in Maryland."

"Do you remember what school that was?"

"Presidio, I think. And all those businesses he said he built up – his experience in finance? They were all fictitious companies."

"Wow."

"Anyway, Kiera was very upset as were some of the other ladies. Dr. Addison and a police officer pulled Austin out of class. I heard he was escorted to his car. Dr. Addison will take over his classes until he can find somebody else."

We chatted for a little longer, while unbeknownst to her, I was bouncing up and down and madly writing notes to Brett. I disconnected and blurted out, "Isn't that where Jarvit, Landry, Cabot, and Shane Buchanan all went? Could he know all of them?"

Brett's hand raked through his hair and he was silent. Then he tapped his fingers on the table, while I not so patiently waited.

"It's possible. We were able to make a clear connection between Cabot and Shane. Like Mrs. Chantilly told you, Cabot moved in with Blake Buchanan in high school. In ninth grade, after his parents were killed in a car accident. No apparent extended family and Blake officially took over guardianship to keep him out of the foster care system."

"That's impressive."

"Both Shane and Cabot were admitted to Presidio College. Shane didn't stay long. He convinced Blake to set him up with the horse farm when it was obvious he was going to fail out. Cabot, however, obtained scholarships and awards. Star student. Went

175

on to get a graduate degree in business from George Washington U and established himself in investments and securities. Cabot is squeaky clean, bonded, and cleared through the Securities and Exchange Commission. They monitor his activity closely."

"Did you ever get the search warrant for his office?"

"Nope. Once the background check and SEC report came through, we were told to back off until we had something besides dinner with old friends."

I shrugged. "That sounds reasonable. The package wasn't being delivered to his house. Wait, did you find anything else on dear sweet Dr. Antos?" I'd already described my earlier interactions with Antos to Brett.

He chuckled. "Leah was quite correct, he got the job fraudulently. No one at Millicent had looked beyond his winning ways and a fake diploma. You'll be happy to know, I made Fabry go get a copy of his application packet and compared it to what we'd already found. More stuff will likely come up, now that we have fingerprints. Dr. Addison was shocked. He talked about how personable Antos was and how he even hand-delivered his transcript. Only the seal on the transcript was fake – not even a good replica of the school he said it was from. But everything looked official and no one checked."

"He used someone good for his papers then."

"That's an understatement. And his references were all fake as well. His business ventures all lies. It was all too neat to be spur of the moment. Antos was too ready to step in and Fabry is suspicious and cynical at heart. He went and checked the records of the faculty member who died. The man had been in bad health for a few years and it was ruled as natural causes. Fabry was disappointed to say the least."

I shook my head. "I can't imagine how Dr. Addison or Antos dealt with being found out. And Dr. Addison was afraid I would put the college in a compromising position. What happened with the meetings this morning? Jarvit and Celeste?"

"Not much with Jarvit. He lawyered up and the lawyer pretty much told Jarvit not to answer any questions Fabry asked unless it was a known fact to anyone. Like the date. Like confirming the Thursday night dinner and the Friday morning breakfast. Like that he knew both Connor and Celeste Landry and Cabot. Fabry worked on him for about an hour trying to wear him down or get him to blurt out something. According to Fabry, his demeanor softened when asked about Celeste. Nothing."

"And Celeste's interview?"

"I did that one and Fabry's correct. She's a looker. Ash blonde hair, blue eyes, and obviously works out. She's not your typical drug addict. She looks healthy, albeit due to make up. Dresses well and takes care in her appearance. I'm not an expert on designer fashion. Clothes looked expensive to me. No surprise, though, she comes from a good family and never lacked for the best."

He took a sip of coffee. "She was cooperative yet restrained. Mourning. Landry didn't have a will. Her explanation of how she and Jarvit ended up at the house was business and trying to sort out businesses. She wasn't aware the open house had been cancelled until he showed up. Then again, she admitted no one had an appointment and walk-ins like Kim were very rare."

"Did you find out anything more about Jarvit or Skinner or the drugs?"

"She's not stupid. She denied any knowledge of drugs. Indicated she had little to do with the businesses, usually just 'arm candy' at meetings or meet-and-greet with potential buyers. She knew what to say about LLC and that it was thriving. The only mis-step was when I asked about her relationship with Jarvit and whether it was all business. Then she faltered. She recovered quickly and explained their relationship as her way to make Landry jealous and nothing serious. When I asked her if Jarvits knew that, her mouth dropped."

"Did Fabry ask Jarvit that question?"

"He asked generally and the attorney conceded that Jarvit and Celeste knew each other through Landry and were business partners."

Brett's phone rang and he scowled – my cue to go check on Maddie and her homework. She was doing well and singing along with a you-tube video. She removed the head phones long enough to tell me "One of the songs for the winter holiday concert. Auditions for solos tomorrow." She put her headphones back on and I went back to the kitchen.

Brett had two wine glasses out and was uncorking a bottle of pinot grigio.

"What's the occasion?" His knitted brows told me this was not a celebration.

"Victoria. After all these months …" His voice was low and he shook his head.

Victoria was his ex-wife and Maddie's mother. She and Roger had moved to Europe before we got married, leaving Maddie in sole custody of Brett. The first year, there was some contact every few months. And then it was longer between contacts.

"What did she want?" I whispered and kept my eye on the hall.

"She wanted to know when Maddie's vacations were. She wants me to send her to Europe."

His grip on the wine glass was turning his hands white and I pried them off. "Before you snap it in two and bleed all over the place. You can fight that, can't you?"

He nodded. "And I'll win. I have no doubt of that. If I can put Victoria off until Maddie's birthday, she'll be sixteen and be able to speak her mind at a hearing if it comes to that."

I wrapped my arms around him. "Did Victoria give any indication of what this was supposed to accomplish? Why she couldn't be bothered to call her daughter?"

"Nope. None. She asked about vacations. I asked why. She wants her to go there and she'll call the school if need be to get the information."

I glanced at our bulletin board with the yearly schedule posted. "Did you tell her?"

"Nope. She wants it, she can do the work to get it. By tomorrow, she may not remember the conversation."

"We can only hope."

We moved to the living room with our wine and turned on the television. Neither of us was really watching it though. All I could think of was what would happen if Maddie decided she wanted to vacation in Europe and how that would affect all of us. After a while, Maddie stumbled out of her room, dogs following behind her.

"What do we have for a snack?"

Brett smiled. "I bet there's still some of those cookies you made. They were pretty good. Maybe you could bring some out on a dish and we could all have a snack."

She smiled and disappeared returning with a plate of cookies and a glass of milk. In between munching, she asked, "Don't you go to the doctor tomorrow about your ankle?"

"Yes. And new x-rays hopefully won't show a break. I really want to walk again. The scooter thing is getting old very fast."

"That's right. I almost forgot about that. Fabry is going to be checking with Skinner about your 'accident' and I'll catch up with him after your appointment. Then we will meet with Jarvis and his attorney again. Maybe with more information thrown at him and a little supposition, his attorney won't be so effective in keeping him quiet."

Maddie cleaned up and went back to her room with Bella. Charlie curled up with us as we finished our wine and cuddled.

CHAPTER 30

With an early morning appointment, we lucked out and Dr. Bregman was running only about twenty minutes late. He sent me for more x-rays and then we waited again. It was worth the wait when Dr. Bergman came in and showed us the x-rays.

"Here's your ankle and there is no indication of a fracture. With the immediate swelling, it's not always possible to tell and the boot was a safety measure. Try putting some weight on it for me."

I stood and tentatively put weight on the foot. "Not too bad."

"Try taking a few steps."

I did, very gingerly. "A little sore."

"Okay. Here's what you need to do. Use the boot and or scooter as needed. In the meantime, for short periods of time, try putting weight on the foot. Gradually increase the time without the boot. If it gets worse, decrease weight bearing, use ice, rest, and your choice of over- the-counter pain medicine. See you in two weeks."

I nodded and he left. Brett and I walked to the elevator. I carried the boot and he carried the scooter. Outside, I used the scooter to the car. Brett dropped me off at the house and I donned the boot. With a little luck, I was able to find a shoe for my right foot with enough of a heel that I wasn't lopsided. As much as I was sick of the boot, I had to admit the support it offered was welcome. Scooter in the passenger seat, just in case, I went to Pets & Paws.

"Hi, Susie. How're all the dogs, today?"

"Good. We homed some of the puppies. New mama, but she hasn't birthed yet. Dr. Barksdale will be by to check on her. Wait, what's with the blue boot? Are you making a fashion statement?"

I chuckled. "Not hardly. Sprained it pretty bad last week. Trying to walk some with the boot for support." Susie disappeared into the mama and pups area as Mrs. Chantilly greeted me.

"Hello, Sheridan. No scooter today? Your foot must be better. Though Brett carrying you over the threshold was so cute. Luke's at school. Sometimes he worries me. He's a good soul, you know. Not like some of those Buchanans."

That was the first time I'd heard her mutter anything negative about a Buchanan recently. "Which one upset you, Mrs. Chantilly? Luke's father?"

"Him and Del, even Lila though I get why she might not visit Shane."

"Has anyone visited Shane since he went to jail?"

"Blake. And each time he gets upset that no one else will visit. This time he checked with the guards. What's wrong with Sebby? Shane was his link to the Buchanans. And his other college friends? Only one of them has been to visit. Sebby owes Shane. If not for him, who knows what would have happened to him."

"Not a lot of people like to go visit people in jail. Usually only the spouse or parents. Does Sebby work up in that area?"

"Of course not. His office is in the southern part of the state. Shane's horse farm was in the northern part of the state. Geography. Even Blake's wife – Shane's mother – hasn't been to visit him. The man is lonely and a ghost of himself. Family is family. I wouldn't desert Blake …"

Ignoring the reference to Blake and family, I tried to find out who the college friend was. "You're very supportive of others, Luke and Lacie and others who have troubles, Mrs. Chantilly. And you did mention at least one friend who visited Shane."

"I always knew Shane was trouble. Sebby would have gone to a foster home. We're having a hard time finding a foster for Cocoa. I hope we can help the poor girl. Help her like Luke and Lacie. Oh, my, I have cookies in the oven."

She turned and shuffled off. I'd noticed her movements getting slower and wondered about her health. On the other hand, we'd just had one of the more lucid conversations since I'd been volunteering at Pets & Paws. I shook my head and texted Brett to check on Shane's visitors. Grabbing a cup of coffee, I got busy with the dogs, Cocoa especially.

I was almost done when I got a text from Kim. She'd spotted Jared Skinner on campus and notified Hirsch. I copied the message to Brett.

The rest of the morning went quickly with only eight dogs to care for. I checked in on Susie before I left. She let me know Mrs. Chantilly had rushed off to lunch somewhere. With Blake, no doubt. I took care of errands and then worked on my lectures for Wednesday.

Over dinner, the conversation focused on the winter concert the week before Thanksgiving. Maddie auditioned for one of the solo spots, as did Alex. I smiled as I recalled the two of them singing together the year before.

"I was so nervous. There were a lot more people and more pressure here at the high school. And I found out, this is partly how Mr. Contralto decides who will be in the show choir – the Chorale – and part of the summer program."

"Were you planning on doing that, Maddie?"

"I don't know that much about it. It's a big honor to be asked though. You have to be good."

I shook my head and Brett asked, "Why is it called a 'show' choir? Do you travel to give shows?"

"Yes and no. It's called a 'show' choir because most of the pieces are from Broadway plays. And, sometimes they do performances at other schools around the state."

"Something to think about then."

"For sure. I told Alex he needs to come visit Pets & Paws and play with Cocoa, Karla, too. I think she'd like the farm, don't you?"

"I don't know and that would be up to Angie. Cocoa takes a while to warm up to people. And to avoid situations like at the corn maze, it would help if she were officially trained as a support animal. Huh. Maybe we could arrange that anyway. It might help her and help her get adopted."

"I know." She picked up dishes and put them in the sink. "Homework." And she disappeared. As Brett and I cleaned up after dinner, I shared with him the high points from my conversation with Mrs. Chantilly.

"I guess I understand how she may think Sebby owes Shane. On the other hand, wouldn't it raise flags given his investment and securities position?"

"Probably. And it could trigger a deeper investigation by the SEC. Or not. It would be a gamble. Fabry is going to visit Shane and check the visitor list. Blake shouldn't have had access to that information."

"I wondered. I guess his name has a lot of clout. It would be interesting to see which of his college friends visited him, when, and how often."

"Fabry is on it. Your good friend Dr. Antos was arrested – he's out on bail, though. A search warrant yielded large quantities of designer drugs, as well as cocaine and other prescription opioids. It didn't take much pressure for him to give up the name of the prescribing physician. That doctor also was charged."

"Did he acknowledge knowing Landry, Jarvit, Cabot or Shane Buchanan?"

"All but Shane. He was a year behind the others, so Shane wasn't around though he admitted hearing the name. He knew about Landry's death and didn't seem particularly upset by it. Didn't have much to say about Jarvit or Cabot. He smiled when he was asked about Jarvit and shrugged at Cabot."

"Anything else? What about the meeting with Jarvit to rile him up? Checking with Skinner?"

Brett groaned. "Meeting with Jarvit was rescheduled to tomorrow. Skinner admitted to knocking you over. Said Jarvit directed him to follow you and send you a message to butt out. That was Skinner's version of 'a message' though he didn't really think you'd been hurt. Up to you whether to press charges."

"I'll think about it. If it ends up he was truly being helpful? I'm a believer of second chances after seeing the difference in Luke."

"He also admitted he threw the brick, again in response to an order from Jarvit. He saved the email." We decided to watch a Hallmark movie and cuddle. Forget about the murder and drugs for a while. Charlie came out to join us and curled up with us.

CHAPTER 31

Dr. Addison was at the door when I arrived and he didn't look particularly happy. He grimaced as I approached.

"I gather your foot is doing better."

"Yes, sir, it is. How are you today?"

"I've had better days. Things will sort out and all will be well. Millicent College will be better when the dust settles."

I nodded and walked past him, wondering at his sour disposition and optimism. Leah wasn't in the lounge and her door was closed. I fell into my normal pattern and was off to teaching. After class, I refilled my coffee and was working on my next class and grading when Leah came in and closed the door.

"Everyone is in an uproar. I think the shock of Monday has worn off. Kiera's aunt is beside herself and Kiera resigned. And is out on sick leave. And the rest of Austin's fan club? They can't say anything good about him. Somehow as they talked about him Monday afternoon and yesterday, they realized how many of them had believed his lies."

"I imagine they are all feeling betrayed and blaming themselves for not seeing through him. Too bad."

"Umm... I tried to distract them and talked about the murder and concerns with drugs. I don't know who talked to whom. The other thing that came down on Monday was a requirement for all the teachers and staff to be trained on types of drugs and an educational program for students. That's happening in English classes. Were you on that email?"

I shook my head. "As a temporary, I'm not on the main listserv. And Mrs. Sinclair must not have remembered to put me in as an add-in. Any comments on that from the rest of the faculty?"

"There were lots of looks and confusion, maybe. We watched the training in groups during off periods yesterday. Dr. Addison kept a list of who attended. Some of Austin's admirers were in my group in the morning, and I saw a few of them pale or clap a hand to their mouth. Kiera was in that group and ran out of the meeting. I think that put her over the top."

Nodding, I picked up my phone and texted Brett. "Other than Kiera, anyone else have an extreme reaction?"

Leah provided me with two other names and I passed them on. Sooner or later, someone would be talking to them. By then, it was time for me to teach my last class. I was thrilled with no scooter on the one hand. On the other hand, my discomfort had imploded to pain. Ibuprofen and home with the foot up was the plan after my class.

I'd fallen asleep on the couch with both dogs and only awoke when Maddie got home. She bounced around the room singing her songs. I smiled.

"Good news?"

She stopped singing and jumped up and down. "Got the solo. Alex, too."

"Congratulations to you both. What about Chorale?"

She sat down on the couch with me, mostly to give the dogs some attention. "He won't make those decisions until January. I'm so excited though. This is a high school performance, you know."

She went on to talk about how high school was so much different than middle school. Inevitably, she got around to the extra rehearsals and the "once I get my license, you or Dad won't have to drive me or pick me up" promotion.

I chuckled and picked up the cold pack off my ankle, returning the foot to the boot. "We need to get the meatloaf in the oven and finish making dinner."

We got everything going and she disappeared back to her room. I checked my messages and worked on grading until Brett came home. After dinner and congratulations again on the solo spot, Maddie disappeared. Brett shared the new information, or at least what he could share, as we cleaned up the kitchen.

"The names you sent me, starting with Kiera? They all dated Antos. When asked about him and drugs, they all acknowledged times when they had dinner with him and felt funny, usually blaming it on the wine or something they ate. After the training and hearing some effects, they wondered if he'd drugged them. The man is total slime. All of them were referred to support services locally and we asked them to share the support services widely."

I cringed. What they must be going through and thinking. Brett interrupted my thinking with more information.

"I did follow-up today with Cabot and his attorney, the focus on what he could tell us about the relationship between Jarvit and both Connor and Celeste Landry. He denied any knowledge of a drug business, acknowledged his suspicion they both used. When asked about Celeste, he smiled. Celeste and he had dated once or twice before she met Connor and married him."

"How'd he feel about that?"

"He seemed okay with it. Cabot describes himself as 'happily married, with two kids, a dog, and the white picket fence' though the fence is actually not white. He had the most traumatic childhood, yet survived."

"You realize, his choice of profession and the structure is probably his way of controlling his future?"

Brett nodded. "True. More to the point, Cabot admitted he'd sensed tension between Landry and Jarvit at dinner. Based on what he said, and the official documents, Landry put up part of the money for Moss Builders and some of the money for Jarvit's real estate office. Cabot figured it was a money thing. He didn't think it was ever a good idea to lend money to a friend. It didn't bode well for the friendship. Have to say, I agree with him on that. He said they were still talking to each other in the parking lot when he left."

"Did he sense anything different with Jarvit at breakfast?"

"He said Jarvit seemed more relaxed and he assumed they had settled their differences."

"What happened with Jarvit's interview? Don't tell me it was rescheduled again."

"Nope. Jarvit's attorney was not a happy camper. This time Fabry's questions were pointed and intended to let Jarvit know it was time to pay up. He started with his relationship with Celeste, assuming she would have already told him what she disclosed. She hadn't."

"What happened?"

"When Fabry asked him about their relationship, Jarvit tried for the business side until Fabry told him she admitted they were having an affair. His attorney answered 'no comment' but when Fabry added that she was having said affair to make her husband jealous, Jarvit lunged for him, yelling about how she loved him, not Landry. It was downhill from there as he tried to make Landry out to be the bad guy and dug himself a very large hole."

He paused and shrugged his shoulders. "The short story is that Landry found out about Jarvit's relationship with Celeste and threatened to pull his money out of Jarvit's business and turn him over to the authorities for drug dealing and distribution. According to Jarvit, Landry dabbled in the drug businesses, mostly as a user, while Jarvit was the prominent one and the one with connections up the line. He was also the only one of the four men who ever visited Shane in jail."

We talked a bit more and settled down with a glass of wine to wait for the official news. It was the big story of the night. Chase Jarvit was arrested in the murder of Connor Landry, with drug charges pending. The next few days included drug busts in Cold Creek, North Shore, Alta Vista, Clover Hill, and the greater Lynchburg area.

EPILOGUE

K im and Marty came up to Clover Hill over the weekend just in time for what now had become a tradition – a picnic in the park with old friends and new. We even sprung Cocoa for a day away from Pets & Paws.

The group was getting larger and more interesting, to say the least, and everyone had questions. With the kids all playing football, the adults made introductions all around and the conversation shifted to the arrest of Chase Jarvit for Landry's murder.

"Can he get out of it? Say the comments he made were under duress?"

Brett shrugged as did Marty and Lee. "The search of his house was finally conducted and though he had lots of time to 'clean' the house, he was arrogant enough to think the search would only uncover obvious things in visible places. In addition to the drugs, a small caliber gun was found that matches the type used to kill Landry. The ballistics test results are still pending verification."

Leah's mouth had dropped at Brett's explanation. "That would surely count for something."

Fabry chimed in. "That gives him means. The drugs are not only part of how he carried it off, but motive. By Jarvit's own report, Cabot threatened to turn him in. On top of that, he was going to pull all his financial backing, not to mention his relationship with Celeste. Opportunity? The last anyone saw Landry was after the dinner, talking with Jarvit. In his ranting, it wasn't clear how he got Landry to the woods, but he had opportunity."

We all nodded. "What about Celeste?"

"Jarvit never implicated her in the murder, she didn't have the gun. She wasn't even living in the house when the package confirmed to be drugs was delivered. She will have a lot to sort out." Fabry laughed before he continued. "She was already wrapping her web around Jarvit's attorney after she asked Cabot for financial advice and he refused."

"Will anything else happen with regard to the drugs?"

"Charges are pending for Jarvit. Several smaller dealers under him and Dr. Antos are being arrested as well."

Leah barely contained herself. "It blew me away when I heard Austin had been arrested, never mind that he didn't have a degree or experience teaching. I mean I figured out he was involved somehow and he gave me the creeps, but, wow, to think I've been working with a con artist and drug dealer all this time. And somehow administration hadn't found that out when they did a background check before he was hired."

"Makes you wonder, doesn't it? I had to be 'cleared' to teach the little ones – even fingerprinted."

I nodded to Melina. "When I worked as a psychologist, I had to be fingerprinted as well. What actually is included in a background check and how effective is it?"

Fabry laughed. "It likely varies. In many cases, the organization or employer asks for a criminal background check that screens for specific problems. In most positions with contact with minors, the question is whether they were arrested for anything indicative of pedophilia or child molestation or child abuse. In a hospital setting, a red flag is often drug charges. For a trucking company, drugs or DUI violations."

"A lot could get missed then?"

"If it's a quick criminal check looking for specific things, then yes. A comprehensive background check is just that – comprehensive. It includes educational records, employment records, and even financial records like credit history. And it's a lot more expensive and takes longer to do."

"Now, we all have to provide a copy of our diploma with each of our degrees." Leah shook her head.

"What better means to have access to students who might be good candidates for designer drugs – or any other drugs?"

"Just plain scary."

"Sheridan, Kim, did you ever decide what to do about Skinner?"

"I gave it some thought and he was helpful in the investigation and following orders. And his 'message' could have been a lot worse than a sprained ankle."

"He agreed to pay for the window and no one was hurt. Sheridan and I discussed it and talked to him. We decided to give him his second chance."

"What about Max and those houses? And all those businesses?" I sure hoped Max wasn't going to lose his house.

Marty chimed in there. "Someone will decide on who owns the Moss Builders and LLC. The homeowners still own the property. The businesses? If the franchise goes under, they have to make a choice to go under or re-establish with a new name and no one supporting them."

"Enough of this. Isn't that a volleyball court over there? Anyone up for a game – adults against kids?" Vanna asked. Being new to the group, she didn't quite get the debrief party after a murder.

Karla and I became the score keepers and cheer leaders, with Cocoa at our feet. It was a good feeling to see everyone enjoying the last few days before the cold of winter. My thoughts sprung to the holidays and arranging some training for Cocoa.

ABOUT THE AUTHOR

About Christa Nardi

Christa Nardi is an avid reader with her love of mysteries beginning with Nancy Drew and other teen mysteries. She especially enjoys cozy mysteries with less gore and no graphic violence. At the same time, she enjoys traditional mystery and crime stories as well. Christa has been a long time writer from poetry and short stories to mystery series. Christa is a member of Sisters in Crime.

You can find Christa Nardi at: Amazon, Goodreads, Twitter, BookBub, Pinterest, and Facebook. You can contact her at cccnardi@gmail.com.
Check out her blog - Christa Reads and Writes
(https://www.christanardi.blogspot)
Check out her website –
(https://cccnardi.wixsite.com/mysite)

Sign up for her monthly newsletter
(https://cccnardi.wixsite.com/mysite/contact)
Follow her on Twitter
(https://twitter.com/ChristaN7777)
Follow her on BookBub
(https://www.bookbub.com/authors/christa-nardi)

Series by Christa Nardi

The Cold Creek Series by Christa Nardi:
Murder at Cold Creek College (Cold Creek #1)
Murder in the Arboretum (Cold Creek #2)
Murder at the Grill (Cold Creek #3)
Murder in the Theater (Cold Creek #4)
Murder and a Wedding (Cold Creek #5)

Sheridan Hendley Mysteries by Christa Nardi:
A New Place, Another Murder (A Sheridan Hendley Mystery #1)
Dogs and More Dogs, Another Murder (A Sheridan Hendley Mystery #2)
Old Friends and New, Another Murder (A Sheridan Hendley Mystery #3)
Holly and Mistletoe, Another Murder (A Sheridan Hendley Holiday Mystery) – coming in 2020

Stacie Maroni Mysteries by Christa Nardi:
Prestige, Privilege & Murder (A Stacie Maroni Mystery #1)
Foundations, Funny Business & Murder (A Stacie Maroni Mystery #2)
Deception, Denial & Murder (A Stacie Maroni Mystery #3)
Connections, Conflict & Murder (A Stacie Maroni Mystery #4)

The Hannah and Tamar Mysteries for Young Adults
with Cassidy Salem:
The Mysterious Package (A Hannah and Tamar Mystery)
Mrs. Tedesco's Missing Cookbook (A Hannah and Tamar Mystery)
The Misplaced Dog (A Hannah and Tamar Mystery)
Malicious Mischief (A Hannah and Tamar Mystery)
Mayhem on the Midway (A Hannah and Tamar Mystery)